THE ISLAND

THE ISLAND

Angie Brijpaul

iUniverse, Inc.
New York   Bloomington

The Island

Copyright © 2009 by Angie Brijpaul

All rights reserved. No part of this book may be used or reproduced by any means, graphic, electronic, or mechanical, including photocopying, recording, taping or by any information storage retrieval system without the written permission of the publisher except in the case of brief quotations embodied in critical articles and reviews.

iUniverse books may be ordered through booksellers or by contacting:

iUniverse
1663 Liberty Drive
Bloomington, IN 47403
www.iuniverse.com
1-800-Authors (1-800-288-4677)

Because of the dynamic nature of the Internet, any Web addresses or links contained in this book may have changed since publication and may no longer be valid. The views expressed in this work are solely those of the author and do not necessarily reflect the views of the publisher, and the publisher hereby disclaims any responsibility for them.

ISBN: 978-0-595-53529-3 (pbk)
ISBN: 978-1-4401-1077-1 (cloth)
ISBN: 978-0-595-63597-9 (ebk)

Library of Congress Control Number: 2008940901

Printed in the United States of America

iUniverse Rev Date: 5/11/2009

For my parents, Nan and Jay

Acknowledgments

Thank you, Nan and Jay Brijpaul, for helping me achieve my dream. I love you both. And to Raynier Maharaj, I express huge gratitude; thank you for reading over my drafts and giving me valuable advice I will never forget.

1

Marie Marcette chewed her lip nervously, brushing back her hair in annoyance. Her hands were grasping the book in front of her so tightly her knuckles had turned a starchy white. Her eyes flickered to the teenager beside her, eyeing him excitedly.

His black hair was unruly, framing his face in a disorderly fashion. Thin, black glasses framed his eyes—the lenses a small square in size—and they seemed to slide off his nose as he scribbled in a book opened to an already filled page.

"I hope I don't have something on my face," the teenager chuckled, and Marie blushed.

"No!" she exclaimed, burning red when she noticed a few people had turned their heads at her outburst.

The teenager smiled at her feeble attempt and held out his hand.

"Julian Summers."

"Marie Marcette." She eagerly took his hand. "Are you here alone?"

Julian closed his book gently, his silver pen wedged between the pages of squiggles. Marie followed his example, placing her book in her lap with a finger to mark the pages.

"Friends, actually. You?"

"Family. My brother won tickets to a resort in the Philippines." Marie glanced down the aisle and caught her eldest brother's nonapproving stare.

She waved happily. As soon as he turned around Marie frowned, looking back to Julian. She shook her head when she saw he had returned to his book, writing fiercely. Marie watched as the flight attendant began to hand out earphones to the passengers. She fiddled with the small screen that was fixed onto the chair in front of her and softly thanked the woman when she received her pair. Sinking back into the lumpy but oddly comfortable chair, Marie tried to watch the badly lit screen and not the teenager beside her.

❁

Jason Kiltez *hated* planes.

The hard, lumpy seats were crawling with bacteria, the cold metal armrests were drowning in germs, and viruses were soaring through the air, and worst of all, he loathed the mushy, uneatable food.

A teenager approached the empty seat beside him, not acknowledging Jason's death stare. Music blared from the headphones strung around his neck, and Jason inwardly groaned at the choice of heavy metal. The teenager glanced at the ticket clutched in his fingerless-gloved hand and then switched his gaze to the tiny sign above the seats. He dropped his black duffle bag on the sticky floor and stiffly lowered himself into the creaky chair, kicking the bag under the seat in front.

The pilot began to address the passengers in a rambunctious voice, which gritted on Jason's nerves. He turned his gaze to the dirt-infested window, staring as the half-dead grass slowly became a speedy blur. Jason dug his nails into his palms as the engine began to roar. He breathed deeply as the plane was knocked against the strong currents of wind, and before long the aircraft was flying smoothly. Jason heard a soft sigh of relief escape the teenager beside him, and he studied the boy from the corner of his eyes.

"Could I help you with something? Or do you just like what you see?"

Jason elegantly raised an eyebrow, a trait he had perfected over many years of practice.

"Excuse me?"

"You're staring."

"So?"

"You're staring at *me*."

"And you have a problem with that?"

"Well, I know it's not something you hear every day, but yes."

This time Jason smirked, and the teenager mirrored his action.

"William Marcette," the teenager said, nodding instead of sticking out his hand.

"Jason Kiltez."

❊

Mark Marcette huffed angrily as his little sister continued to avoid his gaze. He could clearly see the hint of red that stained her cheeks and growled unconsciously, straining in his seat to catch a better look at the teenager beside her.

"Excuse me?" said the girl who sat beside him, looking confused and half-annoyed. "Would you like some brownies? I'm not sure about the food on the plane, but I can guarantee these are tasty."

Mark couldn't help but smile and accept, biting into the chocolaty desert with glee.

"These are good," he said through a mouthful, finishing the brownie in two bites. The girl smiled in response and took several more bites before she was halfway done. Mark wiped his hands on his track pants and quickly held out a hand.

"Mark Marcette. Nice to meet you ...?" His eyes trailed down her long, midnight-colored hair that twisted at her small hips.

"Anitaa. Why the Philippines?"

"Won a contest."

"A radio one?" Mark watched in curiosity as she shuffled through her large handbag and pulled out a wallet. She winked at him and began to dig through the contents before revealing a white ticket laced with gold. "Giving away tickets like this?"

"You're going too?" exclaimed Mark, snatching his ticket from his back pocket.

"You shouldn't put it there," advised Anitaa. "It can easily fall out."

Mark shoved the ticket back into his pocket. "Did you come with your family?"

"My friends. We decided it would be a high school graduation celebration."

Mark grinned when her eyes moved along his figure.

"I bet you're in university. Or college."

"Just finished high school." Mark shuddered as Anitaa leaned closer and inched an eyebrow higher.

"Too bad."

❊

William watched as people pushed and shoved to get off the plane first. He smiled at their impatience and sunk into his seat, waiting until at last the line seemed to trickle into a thin, flowing stream. He grabbed his bag from the sticky floor and hurried down the aisle, refusing to look at the similar teenager who strolled behind him. He made his way past the crowds of people, careful not to touch anyone.

The first stop he made was the bathroom, frantically stripping his gloves and scrubbing his hands until they were a raw red in contrast to the rest of his pale skin. He reached into the inner pocket of his jacket and squeezed a handful of sanitizer; the cool liquid dripped through the cracks of his hand.

Finally, he exited and spotted his sister a couple of feet away, looking through the crowd eagerly. William smiled and quickly cut across the throng of people, grimacing as they brushed past him.

"Will!" Marie wrapped her arms around his waist, squeezing tightly as if they had been separated for more than just a few hours. "This is Julian."

William glanced at Julian before carefully patting the top of her head with his half-gloved hand.

"Is this your brother?" Julian asked and then smiled when he got no answer.

There was a quiet cough behind them, almost as if someone was clearing their throat for attention, and they all turned. Jason nodded to Julian and dropped his bag by their feet. He pointed toward a section of streaming people, and Julian saw a hint of curly hair.

"There's Antonio and Anitaa," said Jason.

Antonio had a pair of sunglasses pushed into his chestnut curls. A thin sheen of sweat had his shirt sticking to his skin. He gave them a bright smile and lowered his bag to the ground. Anitaa followed his gesture and yawned.

"Hey guys, how was the flight?"

"Antonio!" a musical voice called out, and a woman walked briskly toward the friends, clutching the sleeves of two teenagers. Her curls resembled Antonio's, only hers were longer in length and held a healthier shine. "These are my children, Diego and Salatina. I told you about them on the plane, remember? My twins." She released their clothing and smiled broadly. "If we're going to be spending a week together, then you all should be making friends."

"Mom!" the girl—Salatina—complained.

Mrs. Razat waved and then turned elegantly, heels clicking against the tiled floor. As soon as she left another teenager, straw-colored hair with a face decorated with freckles, wobbled toward them.

"Sandy!" Anitaa cried.

William scrunched up his nose as the smell of musty tang invaded his senses.

"What reeks?" asked Diego before he and his sister broke into a round of giggles.

"Shut it," mumbled Sandy. He was blushing. "Some stupid moron stuck my fingers in a water bottle when I fell asleep. The sucker was gone before I woke up."

"I wonder who that smart fellow was," Diego muttered.

William was sure he saw a smirk on the teenager's lips before their eyes met briefly.

A man in a trimmed and tailored suit approached the group, sunglasses pushed into his hair and a cheery, fake smile glued to his face. "Welcome, welcome, everyone, to the Philippines! Is everyone here?" Adjusting his suit the man gave a perfunctory glance around the room. "Good, good! I'm Jim Slate, and I'll be taking you all to your hotel!"

It was midsummer in the Philippines, and the weather was hot and humid, a sweltering combination. The air was sticky, as though they had just walked through a gigantic spiderweb. The group's skin quickly became glossy from sweat with just a short walk from the airport to the bus.

"All right, everyone," called Slate as he stood on the steps. His head barely reached Mark's shoulder. "I just need to make sure we've got everyone. Let me just quickly count heads." Slate's expression drastically changed to nervousness as he glanced at the paper he held and then at the people who stood in front of him, fatigued but excited. He ran a hand through his short, greasy hair before dropping the fantastically fake smile.

"Uh, e-excuse me, everyone?"

Murmurs rang through the air as the large group slowly began to listen to the now stuttering man. He glanced at the paper, and his eyes quickly darted past everyone.

"Is something wrong?" one of the adults asked.

"No … Well, yes." Slate tried to smile reassuringly before he dropped the façade. "There's supposed to be fourteen of you. Someone's missing."

2

The crowd froze as one, each face wearing a different expression. Mrs. Marcette gasped as she turned in a circle. Her short, blond hair bobbed against her shoulders with her movement, and as she completed her circle her expression of concern grew.

"Will?" she called hesitantly. Her brow creased with worry, making her face seem older and more vulnerable.

"I'm here," William muttered. "Quit yelling; I was only gone for a second." His head popped out from behind a suitcase. "No worries, and all that crap." He pushed his way to the front, elbowing Jason to get past him.

"You're all right?" Slate asked as he wrung his hands together.

"Looks that way, doesn't it? Can I go in the bus now?"

Slate, appearing stunned, stepped aside, and William vanished past the metal doors. Mrs. Marcette hurriedly approached the man, glaring at the white speckled bus.

"I'm so sorry," she said, "he's not normally like this."

"Of course he is," said Marie. She ignored the blank stares directed at her and followed her brother onto the bus.

After a few hours, the vehicle stopped in front of a middle-class hotel, not very luxurious looking but still maintaining an elegance most cheap hotels were short of. The building seemed to be in the middle of nowhere, and the only thing that looked remotely alive was the green vines twisting down the hotel's gigantic columns.

Marie stared out the grimy window, finger tracing the coiling vines on the cloudy glass. As they exited the bus in a staggered line, Marie couldn't help stare at Slate's greasy smile. She felt a shudder flicker through her body when their eyes connected briefly. He bowed his head, his oily hair hanging limply, and Marie quickened her pace. Something was off about that man—Jim Slate—something was definitely not right.

※

"Can we, Mom? It's right across the hall!" Marie begged.

Mrs. Marcette smiled and looked at the two girls for a few minutes before she slumped her shoulders in an exaggerated gesture. "Fine, Marie, you've broken me down." She laughed, ruffling her daughter's hair as she looked the pair over. "Do you two want to stay here or in Salatina's room?"

Marie exchanged looks with Salatina, and they both grinned. She didn't have to ask to know what Salatina was thinking.

"Salatina's?"

Mrs. Marcette nodded, and Marie beamed, hugging her mother tightly around her waist. "Thank you!"

"And there are enough beds?"

Marie nodded and waved to her parents, linking her arm around Salatina's and pulling her out of the small room.

"Bye, Will!" she shouted over her shoulder and heard a crash in response.

Salatina knocked on the door opposite to the Marcette's room. It opened slightly, and Diego stuck his head out. He grinned at the two with a boyish charm and wiggled his eyebrows. "Why, hello, ladies," he said in a deep tenor, winking at Marie.

Salatina rolled her eyes and pushed the door open, banging Diego into a wall as she passed.

"Hey!" he squealed, his voice no longer ridiculously low. He rubbed his left arm and pouted. "Don't hurt me; I bruise like a banana!"

"We're sharing a room."

"We are?"

"Not me and you. *Not* you and Marie. Marie and *I* are sharing a room."

"Oh, okay." Diego bobbed his head and followed the girls to the farthest door.

"I'm already unpacked, but I can help you," said Salatina.

Diego moved closer and stretched his arm around Marie's shoulder, tilting his head to touch hers. "Me too. Where's the underwear?"

Marie froze, feeling her heartbeat quicken and cheeks burn red. "Diego!" she shrieked and shrugged out of his embrace in embarrassment.

Diego laughed loudly and quickly blew her a raspberry kiss as Salatina shooed him out the door.

"Sorry about that. He can be such an idiot sometimes."

Marie smiled at Salatina and shrugged, not minding Diego's playful nature. "Yes, but he's a *cute* idiot. Just don't tell him I said that."

"Don't worry," Salatina stated firmly, reaching into the suitcase for more clothing. "I have no intention of mentioning it."

❉

"Jason, quit being difficult! There's no room left!" Anitaa pleaded.

"Then why doesn't one of you leave if you feel so strongly?" Jason glowered at the three, sending his angriest look toward Sandy.

The blond sneered in response, stepping closer to Jason before Antonio stopped him with an outstretched hand.

"Jason, there's been some mix-up with the rooms! Julian doesn't mind; Diego's helping him unpack right now! Just swallow your pride and go ask the Marcette's—you can share with Mark or Will—I'm sure they wouldn't mind!"

Jason scowled and slammed the door shut, slumping in the hallway. He sighed and faced the door opposite him, raising a hand tentatively. He knocked slowly, swallowing the vile of anger in his throat as the green door creaked open.

"Mrs. Marcette."

"Jason? Is there something wrong?"

"I need a room. There doesn't seem to be enough space."

Mrs. Marcette smiled as she stepped aside, ushering Jason in.

"Not enough rooms?" she asked as she knocked on a closed door.

"Apparently not enough for me or Julian."

"Does Julian need a room too? Mark and William were originally going to share, but …"

"He's staying with the Razats."

Mrs. Marcette nodded and opened the door. A low bass could be heard blaring from the headphones around William's neck. He looked up calmly, giving Jason an odd glance.

"Jason is going to be sharing with you, Will."

"Whatever," said William as he shoved his music player into his pocket. He left the room, ignoring the frustrated expression that danced across his mother's wrinkled face.

❋

Julian raised his cup of tea to his lips and took in the wondrous smell. He savored the bittersweet taste and sighed contentedly, trying to relax his tense muscles. He set the cup on the grimy countertop and then ran his fingers through his untamable hair, glaring at the book sprawled in front of him. He set his pen beside the book and clutched the steaming mug with both hands, trying to think clearly.

"Julian, honey," Mrs. Razat called out, gliding gracefully into the kitchen. Her curls were pinned atop her head, framing her glowing face elegantly. Her soft hands fluttered to his shoulders, and she rubbed them in a motherly way. Julian liked to imagine his mother had been like Mrs. Razat, caring and nurturing in every way possible—not broken and lifeless like he remembered. "Carlos and I are going for groceries. Can you get the children and join the Marcettes? I don't want you all to be alone."

Julian nodded, smiling into his mug as she attempted to tame his unruly hair. She gave up after a few seconds of battling with the wild tresses, patting his shoulders once more.

"Thank you so much, my dear," she exclaimed, as Mr. Razat emerged from a closed door, a bright pink purse hanging from his shoulder.

"Julian," he greeted.

Julian smiled briefly and waved as the Razats hurried out the door, arguing with a light tone in Spanish. He quickly made his way to the girls' room and knocked quietly, waiting a moment before opening the door.

Marie gasped in surprise and squeaked as her foot got caught in a tangle of clothes. Julian blinked as she crashed to the ground, and in seconds, her face flushed to a beet red. The twins' laughter erupted simultaneously, something that seemed to be a common occurrence between the two. Julian looked at his filled hands before managing to wiggle his book under his armpit and stretch a hand toward Marie, pulling her to her feet.

"Your parents are gone grocery shopping. They wanted us to go to the Marcette's room."

The trio exchanged a look before following Julian out the door, through the kitchen, and into the murky hallway. The twins looked at Marie and tapped their foot.

"What?" asked Marie.

Salatina huffed and gestured to the closed door that loomed in front of them. Diego's elbows were planted on his hips, and his head was cocked to the side, fingers tapping to the same rhythm as his foot.

"The key?"

Marie's jaw dropped slightly, and she quickly dug into her back pocket, pulling out the wobbly card. The door swung open with its usual high-pitched scream, and Marie ushered everyone in.

William sat with his feet propped on the sullied table, music blasting from the tiny speakers that hung around his neck.

"Where are Mom and Dad?"

"Groceries."

"Them too?" Diego asked before casually slinging a hand around Marie. He grinned at Salatina and then noticed William, swiftly snapping his arm away from Marie and lowering it to his side.

William laughed amusedly. "I don't care. I'm not Mark."

Marie smiled and grabbed Diego and Salatina's arms and pulled them through the open door.

William nodded behind him, already beginning to make his way to one of the other doors. "I'll be in my room."

Julian sighed, happily taking a sip of his green tea and setting it beside him. He took a seat so he faced the rooms and not the front entrance before lowering his book and opening it to the desired page. He heard the door creak open slowly and the person hesitate before stepping into the room.

"What are you doing?"

Julian glanced behind him and nodded a greeting to Mark. The teenager was coated in sweat and had a thick, white towel thrown over a shoulder.

"Writing."

"You write books?"

"Yes." Julian carefully shut his book when he noticed Mark peering over his shoulder and turned toward the teenager.

"Have any been published?"

"Yes."

"How many?"

"Six or seven," said Julian in a bored voice, knowing that he had published plenty more than that. But what Mark didn't know couldn't hurt him.

"Oh." Mark shifted, obviously uncomfortable as time trickled by at an unbearably slow pace. He shifted under Julian's intense stare before pointing behind him, already taking small steps backward. "Well, I'm going to go down to the gym now. Bye." As soon as he turned, Julian chuckled. "Hey, what's so funny?"

"Well, surely you didn't come in here to talk to me," Julian replied, raising one of his eyebrows in clear amusement. "I think you're forgetting your water."

❁

Marie and Salatina emerged from behind the dark oak door, slinking into the kitchen silently. Julian was standing by the counter, pouring something into a tall mug. Salatina elbowed Marie and wiggled her eyebrows before both broke out into giggles. Julian looked up in surprise.

"Hello, ladies." He smiled and adjusted his glasses.

"Hi," Marie said shyly.

Diego opened the door and threw Marie's key toward her. He was grinning mischievously as he roped an arm around his sister's neck.

"It's all done, Salamander," he said with a chuckle.

"Diego!" Salatina growled, and he sniggered, moving his head and missing her fist by a few inches.

The doorknob began to rattle, and after a minute Mark walked in, glistening in sweat. Marie pinched her nose and swatted her hand through the air. "Ew, Mark! Take a shower. You stink!"

Julian chuckled and then quickly scribbled in his book. He gulped the remainder of his tea and set the cup down in the sink. Just as he was turning around, a pounding at the door startled them. Salatina was the one who strode to the door and glanced through the peephole.

"It's just Antonio."

As soon as she opened the door, Antonio ran into the room and scurried behind Mark. Sandy, his face wrinkled in anger and a small bottle clutched in his hand, followed before Salatina could close the door. A hat had been hastily pulled over his hair.

"I can't believe you! You—"

"What is it this time?" a bored voice interrupted, and Sandy turned around. Jason was standing behind him with his usual smirk.

"He put dye in my shampoo!" Sandy pointed an accusing finger at Antonio.

Marie noticed Diego make an effort to hide his grin and caught Salatina's eye. Marie elbowed Diego gently and whispered, "I know you had something to do with this."

"Just wait till you see the color."

Anitaa followed Jason into the room and hurried toward Sandy. Her expression was sympathetic. "It can't be that bad, Sandy."

Sandy glared at Antonio before reaching up to grasp the hat, allowing his newly dyed locks to fall free. The silence was broken by giggles that came from the direction of the twins.

"It's not funny!" Sandy snarled, shoving the hat back on his head.

"I beg to differ," Jason smirked. "Nice color choice. Thought you'd go for hot pink instead of lime green, but whatever floats your boat."

"He dyed my hair green!"

"I didn't do anything!" said Antonio. "I woke up to see this guy standing over me, screeching like a banshee!"

A loud rumble interrupted the argument, and all eyes turned to Marie. She groaned in embarrassment and placed a hand on her stomach. "Sorry, I'm just hungry."

Diego nodded in agreement and headed to the refrigerator. "Me too. Last time I had food—if you can call it that—was on the plane." He opened the fridge door and poked his head in. Clearly surprised, he shut the door and turned around.

"Diego?"

"There's nothing!" he cried, running over to check the cabinets.

"Diego?" Salatina asked again as her brother slid down the cabinet doors. The floor was now littered with pots and pans of all sizes. Diego buried his face in his hands and moaned loudly. Marie suspected he was a very melodramatic teenager.

"There's no food here!" he cried. "We're going to starve!"

3

Marie flinched when she heard the slap echo through the room. Her eyes possessed a trace of sympathy as she gazed at the red spot rapidly appearing on Diego's cheek. Diego was staring at his sister in shock. His mouth resembled a carp's as it opened and closed without a single sound emerging.

"What the hell was that for?" he finally blurted out.

Salatina released a string of words in Spanish that caused both Diego and Antonio to blush.

"Antonio, what are they saying?"

Julian cleared his throat, interrupting Antonio's answer. "I'm sure I said your parents went out for groceries."

"You did," said Salatina. She glared at her brother. "He's just being dramatic."

Julian shrugged and waved halfheartedly as he exited the room, leaving the rest of them to stare pointedly at Diego's embarrassed form.

Marie headed toward her two friends, her smile brightening as she got closer. "You know, Diego, if you had just listened, this whole matter could've been avoided."

The lights attached to the walls flickered every so often, and every corner Julian spotted was decorated with silky webs. The walls were tinged with grime but seemed to maintain an eerie elegance with their rich, oaky color.

His wet hair blocked a fraction of his vision as he strayed down the dwindling hallway. A familiar pattern of clicks echoed behind him, and Julian slowed his pace, immediately recognizing the footsteps.

"Have you seen William?"

Julian sighed, annoyed to see manners were once again a thing of the past. "No." Julian followed Jason into the elevator and peered at the buttons. "Maybe we should check the library."

"I was getting to that," Jason huffed.

Julian nodded and felt the elevator slow to a stop. They got out, Jason gently pulling him along as he gazed in inquisitiveness. Julian moved toward a large stack of books when a hand clasped his shoulder suddenly and drew him back.

"We're searching for William, not looking through books."

Julian shrugged away from the grip.

"Didn't you hear me?" Jason sneered in annoyance.

"Oh, I heard you, all right," Julian muttered. "I'm sure everyone heard you." He smiled lightly, picking up an old book and blowing the dust off it. He opened it in the middle and ran a hand over the pages. "He's up there."

❈

Marie dug into the pasta with renewed frenzy and smiled in pleasure as the sauce melted in her mouth, the delightful taste returning every time she licked her lips. She turned to grin at Mark but saw he was too busy glaring at someone in the doorway. Wondering who it was, she turned her head and dropped her spoon in surprise. The loud clang it made caused some of the others to jump, and Marie felt her cheeks begin to burn.

"I hope I'm not intruding," Julian announced. "I went to the other room first, but no one was there so …"

Mrs. Razat stood—her face shinning as usual—and quickly approached the teenager. Her curls had been let down and cascaded over her shoulders, coiling down her back and resting near her hips.

"Nonsense, Julian! Please, join us." She took his arm and led him to an empty seat.

"How'd you get in?" Mark demanded.

"William lent me his card when he and Jason left the library; they said they were going to look around before coming here." Julian thanked Salatina as she passed him a plate, and he began to select his food.

"Marie made the sauce," Diego piped up.

"It looks delicious!"

"Th … thanks." Marie shot Diego an annoyed glance before fidgeting with the tablecloth once again.

The door opened, and William entered, followed closely by Jason. Both were sporting an amused smirk. William took the empty chair beside his sister, leaving Jason to take the seat beside Sandy.

"I thought Julian had your card," said Mark suspiciously.

Jason and William chuckled together.

"We got another card from the secretary in exchange for something." Jason grinned at Julian. "Julian has a date tomorrow."

Julian choked on his water. "What?" he and Marie exclaimed simultaneously.

"A date?" Julian's voice was oddly high.

"Tomorrow. At eight. Have fun."

Antonio pushed his chair back, and the wooden legs screeched against the tiled floor with a high wail. He walked to the fridge and grabbed a can of whipped cream and a covered tray. He closed the door with his foot and made his way back to the table. He put the whipped cream down with a soft *clunk* and opened the tray, revealing a custard-looking desert.

"What exactly is that?" Sandy asked.

"Flan!" both Diego and Salatina yelled out in excitement, before Antonio could answer. Antonio grinned as they eagerly held out their plates.

Sandy continued to stare at the dessert. "I still don't know what it is."

"A Spanish dessert," Jason supplied.

Dinner finished shortly after, and Julian, despite Mrs. Marcette and Mrs. Razat's wishes, insisted on doing the dishes and even managed to secure Jason's help. Together, the two acted as a familiar team, effectively taking, washing, drying, and putting the dishes away in an hour.

When they finally returned to their chairs, a lazy atmosphere had settled over the group. Mr. Razat and Mr. Marcette shared a look of amusement before Mr. Razat cleared his throat and stood, demanding the attention of the room.

"We have some great news …"

"And before we tell you, *everyone* is going, no exceptions," interrupted Mrs. Marcette, fixing a pointed look at William and Jason. The two teenagers glared in response.

"The front desk told us this was included with our trip!" exclaimed Mrs. Razat. "Guess where we're going?"

"The zoo?" asked Marie.

"The beach?" asked Anitaa.

"Home?" asked Jason.

"Think harder."

"Can't you just tell us?" asked Diego.

Salatina dug her elbow into his ribcage. "Be patient," she admonished before turning to her mother. "So? Are you going to tell us?"

"You don't practice what you preach," Diego muttered, rubbing his side. He turned to his parents. "Well? Are you? What about now?"

"Or now?" asked Salatina.

"Or …"

"Now?"

Mrs. Razat ran a hand through her curls in exasperation. A smile burst through the tension in her face, and she clapped her hands joyfully, her mood quickly changing. "Scuba diving!" she announced. "We are all going scuba diving!"

4

Jason frowned at the browning ceiling as the sun glared down on his face. He huffed and rolled over, pulling at the covers as he mumbled grumpily. Sighing, he glanced at the clock on the wall and cringed when he saw the time. Six in the morning; no one in their right mind would be awake yet.

Moaning inwardly, Jason regretfully removed the warm blankets and sat up. As he looked around the room, he noticed William's bed was already made. He rolled his eyes, wondering what was wrong with the teenager.

Jason walked over to the bathroom and scowled at his bed hair. He pressed it down with his hands and growled again as it sprang back up. After brushing his teeth, he stumbled to his suitcase, trying to find something decent to wear before heading to the kitchen. He walked to the coffeepot and blinked when he saw coffee had already been made. He poured the black liquid into the tallest mug he could find, not bothering to add milk or sugar. He sighed in satisfaction when he took a gulp of the drink, watching hazily as William approached him and grabbed the coffeepot.

Jason returned the look and snatched the pot back from the surprised teenager. He poured the coffee from his mug back into the pot, and without a word, he walked, pot in hand, into the corridor, letting the door swing shut on its own. He was pleasantly surprised to see Julian slumped against the wall. He glanced at the mug next to the scribbling teenager, certain that it held Julian's green tea. He took another large gulp from the pot, taking care not to spill any of the coffee on his shirt.

"I don't know how you can drink that stuff; it's so plain," Julian muttered, not sparing Jason a look. He scrunched his nose and shook his head.

Jason almost laughed at the sight; whenever Julian wiggled his nose, Jason was reminded of a bunny. "And I don't know how you can stand *that* stuff; it has no taste."

Julian closed his book and smiled. He raised his mug and chuckled, lifting a hand to adjust his glasses. "Touché," he replied, and Jason held up the coffeepot with a smirk. The two clanked the objects together before swallowing their drinks of choice. Julian ran a hand through his messy hair. His expression was filled with drowsiness, and Jason figured Julian must have just woken up; his eyes looked as though they were struggling to stay open.

"Why are you out here?"

Julian just moved his shoulders slightly, holding his empty cup toward Jason.

Jason smirked as he poured the black liquid into the cup and watched Julian take a long sip. "I thought you didn't drink coffee."

Julian drained the cup. He smiled and stretched his limbs with a grimace. "I don't."

❖

The harbor smelled of fish—lots and lots of fish. The place did not seem the safest, but it held a certain quality that drew people in. The soothing sound of the waves brushing against the docks was calming, and every now and then, a small spray of water would fly into the air, and the wind would catch it in a refreshing breeze. Boats of all sizes were tied to the docks, floating gently on the calm water. They bobbed up and down rhythmically in an odd set of patterns.

As the group of fourteen stretched their cramped muscles, a rugged-looking man approached them. A small stubble was apparent, and his hair was tussled with thick tangles weaved into the locks. His eyes were a stormy gray, and his face was crinkled and worn by time. Oddly enough, a small chunk of his ear was missing near the top, but the wound appeared to be old and shabby and must have happened in his younger days.

"Hello, everyone! I assume you all are the fourteen ticket winners?" A couple of nods spurred him on. "My name is Thomas Derka, and I'll be your scuba diving instructor. I'll be taking you all across the waters to an island called Isle de Cala. If you'll all follow me, I'll show you to our boat for the day." His voice was rough, much like his appearance. It seemed to fit him perfectly.

The group followed Thomas as he led them to a two-level boat. They made their way to the front, and Thomas motioned at a man watching the waves with a wary eye.

He was older than Thomas; that was for sure. His hair was a mixture of black and silver, and his face was creased with endless lines. A few scars streaked his face, and his skin looked almost waxy despite the bright sunlight that shone down on them.

"Everyone," said Thomas, "this is our captain, Mr. Stone. He has been sailing for over twenty years. He'll be taking us to our destination today."

Stone glanced at the sky and shook his head. Instead of greeting the crowd, he just shoved past them and made his way to the lower deck. Thomas appeared taken aback before he shook the incident off and smiled at them all, rubbing his hands together enthusiastically.

"All right, folks, we'll be leaving in ten minutes."

※

William worriedly stared at the darkening sky. He could almost smell the rain in the air. He shivered but ignored the cold, preferring to stare blankly into the bleak waters below.

"There you are!" Mark said as he walked toward William. "Great, you're freezing too. And I just gave my sweater to Marie."

"Take mine."

The two siblings shifted in the direction of the scruffy voice. Jason stood there, shrugging off his coat to reveal a thick, black turtleneck.

"Th … thank you," William stuttered.

The others were sitting next to each other on a couple of beat-up-looking couches when the trio made their appearance on the lower level. William made to sit by his mother, but a sudden lurch from the boat threw him off balance.

"What was that?" Salatina asked from the floor. The boat tilted again, causing the standing passengers to stagger.

"Stone!" Thomas exclaimed and climbed the stairs two at a time. He was followed by everyone, as he ran toward the captain's slumped body. The limp man was supported by the steering wheel, which looked like it was about to snap under his weight.

"What's wrong with him?" Salatina asked.

Mrs. Marcette pushed her way to the front. "Let me through; I'm a doctor!"

With Thomas's help, she lowered the captain off the steering wheel and onto his back. Stone was shaking violently, and his limbs twitched every so often. His eyes fluttered, and only the whites could be seen. Mrs. Marcette quickly checked Stone's pulse near his neck. Her eyes flashed worry, but her tone remained calm and firm as she pronounced, "He's having a stroke."

The boat slanted drastically as the steering wheel began to spin. Antonio grabbed it and struggled to keep it under control. He gritted his teeth as the wheel seemed to fight back.

The weather had changed suddenly, and now they were in a violent downpour. The rain crashed against the deck's wooden planks with fury, and the wind howled with no remorse. Some of the teenagers rushed out to the open deck, anxious to see what was happening. The sky was now black, and the clouds had formed a giant veil of darkness. Most of the oxygen tanks had fallen out of the boat, but a few were left, and they were rolling around the deck dangerously.

William grabbed the railing as the boat roughly pitched forward. Julian collided with the railing next to him. They exchanged looks and began to hurry back to the adults when another vehement wave struck the vessel, causing both to slam against the slippery, metal railing once more. Julian had suddenly reached over the railing when another wave hit, and William had to grab Julian's shirt and haul him back, or the teenager would have tumbled over the rail.

"Are you crazy?" William shouted over the rumbling.

Julian yelled something that was muffled by the wind and then pointed to his eyes. His glasses were missing, now swallowed by the churning waters below.

A shrill scream pierced the clamor as Anitaa pointed toward the waves. "Rocks!" she shrieked. "We're headed straight for rocks!"

William glanced over the side just in time to see the sharp, pointy ends of wet stone, before the boat abruptly twisted to one side.

"Sandy!" Anitaa screeched suddenly.

William turned swiftly and froze, and suddenly everything seemed to play out in slow motion.

Sandy never saw it coming. A rolling tank slammed into his heels, and Sandy buckled over the side of the boat and into the raging waters below.

5

Before Jason could dive in after Sandy, Mark curled his fingers around his arm in a bruising grip and pulled him aside. Jason struggled in vain.

"What the hell do you think you're doing?" both roared in anger.

Jason attempted to free himself, but Mark tightened his grip.

"I could save him!" cried Jason. He turned his head to the murky ocean, but Sandy had already vanished from view.

"You can't! There are rocks down there!" A sudden jolt caused Mark to grab the railing with one hand, steadying himself and Jason. "He could be dead already!"

Jason glanced around the boat, his body in a numb state of shock. Anitaa clutched Julian's shoulder, sobbing desolately in the rain, while Julian stood, frozen in shock and fear. His eyes came to rest on Antonio's broken figure, knees on the ground and hands covering his face. Everyone seemed to have seen the whole pain-stricken incident.

Mrs. Marcette suddenly looked up from the captain. Her fingers were gently pressed against his wrists. She looked at her husband and then quickly reached for Stone's neck, resting her fingers against the side.

"He's dead."

A loud bang echoed throughout the boat before the steering wheel began to turn at a lightning speed.

Thomas ran out onto the deck, ignoring the raging weather. "We're all going to die!"

Marie immediately flung herself into William's chest, weeping wretchedly. She squeezed her eyes shut, and her body began to shake. She felt an arm around her shoulder and glanced up. Mark drew them closer.

What happened next took only a few seconds. An earsplitting screech echoed off the boat, sending shivers down their spines—a morbid melody that foreshadowed their death. Rocks scratched against metal like long, broken nails dragged against a rusty chalkboard. Quivers coiled through skin as apprehension swirled around the air.

No one moved to stop the steering wheel.

Antonio began to whisper in Spanish, and Mrs. Razat joined him, clasping his hand and squeezing it gently. Her eyes twinkled with unshed tears, but a smile was still present on her pale lips.

William slipped out of his family's embrace and raced toward the railing at the front of the boat.

"Will!" Marie cried, staring at her brother in surprise.

William ignored Marie and grabbed the drenched railing, watching the rocks as they neared at a maliciously slow pace. Tight fingers wrapped around his arm and he twisted around.

"What do you think you're doing?"

William pushed Jason's hand away and struggled against the teenager. "I'm not going to wait here to die! I'm taking my chances!" Before anyone could stop him, William clambered onto the slippery rail and dived into the rampant ocean. With Mark not there to stop him this time, Jason followed the teenager into the powerful waters without a second thought.

"William!" Marie screamed in anguish. She beat her fists against Mark's chest, begging him to let her go.

Julian sagged against Antonio, staring at where Jason had stood mere seconds ago. Antonio supported Anitaa and Julian, his strong arms stopping the two from crumbling to the floor.

"Guys?" he whispered quietly and pressed his forehead against theirs. "I'm glad I got to know you. You're the best friends a guy could have."

Julian glanced at him, his eyes crinkled with tears. He grasped Antonio's forearm and squeezed it, and Antonio returned the gesture.

Anitaa grabbed Antonio and pulled him into a rough, passionate kiss. They parted at the same time, and she offered a sad smile but no explanation.

"Mom?" asked Diego. "It was me who put your good dress in the dishwasher."

Mrs. Razat sniffed and pulled him closer. "I forgive you," she said quietly.

"And Dad, I used your shoe as a plunger, not Sal."

Mr. Razat twitched slightly but wrapped his arms around Diego and Salatina. "And I forgive you."

"And Sal," Diego said quietly, "I ate the cookies you made for Aunt Liv."

"I know. I baked laxatives into them, remember?"

Diego winced. "Yes."

Salatina smiled and kissed him on the cheek. "You're the best twin ever."

"You're not too bad yourself."

An instant later, the boat sank into the icy waters, and the passengers went with it.

❊

Marie's eyes opened with a sudden burst of energy, and she gasped. Her fingers curled into the ground, and she began to cough violently, shaking as her body was rattled. Her wet hair clung to her face, and clumps of sand stuck to her trembling body.

A soft wave washed over her, and she panted for air again, struggling to keep her head above water. She braced herself for the pain and sat up, swaying nauseously. Tentacles of seaweed were wrapped around her legs, binding the limbs. She tore through them and backed away from the ocean, wheezing in exhaustion. She grasped the slick surface of the nearest rock and pulled herself shakily to her feet, hanging on to the rock for balance. Her forehead felt slimy, and something was trickling down the side of her face. She brought a hesitant hand toward her skin and licked her dry lips in fear. When she pulled away, her fingers were coated in blood. She looked around, only seeing sand, water, and trees. She began to slowly clamber over moss-colored rocks and pieces of shattered wood assumed to be debris from the boat.

In the distance, she could make out the tip of something brown and fuzzy, and as she got closer, she realized it was hair. She hitched a tiny breath when she realized who the hair belonged to.

"Diego?"

He was propped beside one of the larger rocks, his moving chest indicating he was still breathing. Marie gazed at his torn clothes and bloodied skin. She fell to her knees, wincing when the sand mixed with her open cuts. She crawled until she could reach him, and she shook his shoulders as gently as she could.

"Diego!"

He stirred slightly before groaning, shocking Marie as he turned his face to reveal a long, jagged cut across his cheek. She raised her hand to inspect it but pulled away at the last moment. His eyes fluttered open slowly, and she rubbed his arm, attempting to bring him to his senses.

"Diego?" she asked as she grasped his hand. "Are you all right?"

He coughed brutally before laying his head against the rock and closing his eyes once more.

"Marie?" He weakly smiled when she nodded and sat beside him. "I crawled here," he mumbled. "Give me a minute."

"How're you feeling?"

Diego frowned before he squeezed her hand in reply. "Like I almost died out there." He shuddered before facing her and cringed at the blood that caked her forehead. "We'd better take care of that."

Marie nodded and touched his cheek gently, her finger just above his nasty cut. "You're hurt."

"It's nothing," he responded. "Tear my sleeves; we can use them as bandages"

Marie reached for the ragged edge of her long skirt instead. She handed the strip to him, and he gently tied it around her head.

"Do your legs burn?" Marie asked suddenly.

Diego paused with his knot. "What?"

Marie gestured to the pattern of dotted holes that coiled around his shins and disappeared above his knees. "Do they burn?" she repeated as she lifted her skirt a little. "Because mine do."

❈

Julian panted as he slumped to the sand, trying to breathe deeply but failing. He closed his eyes and raised a hand to his face in an attempt to block out the blistering sun. He watched as red droplets slowly fell onto the sand, creating a disgusting, grainy texture. He sighed wearily before turning behind him to face Mr. Marcette.

"I can't do this anymore," he said, wheezing.

"We can't stop."

Julian could feel something drip down the side of his head, but he wasn't sure whether it was sweat or blood.

"I can't," Julian repeated, as he breathed heavily.

"You rest here, then. I'll just have a quick look around the place."

Julian watched Mr. Marcette jog into the forest behind them. He turned to the ocean and squinted, seeing something move in the distance.

"Is anybody there?" Julian called out and struggled to rise, hobbling toward the rocks in front of him. He sat on the closest, stretching his leg out and hissing at the pain that followed. Something to the side caught his attention, and Julian leaned forward, straining to see.

"Oh god," he whispered in horror before scrambling back in distress. His hand slipped from the stone, and he tumbled to the ground, slamming his head against the rocks that littered the sand. He felt a short burst of pain and then nothing.

6

Thomas groaned and shivered from the cruel, whipping wind. He had crawled into a small cavern hours before, deciding it would best serve as a shelter. He had yet to eat but couldn't stand the thought of food after nearly drowning; his stomach was still recovering from the vomit that lay a few feet away.

He clambered further into the hole and frowned wearily, fearful of the darkened shadows. He edged forward, and the ground underneath him gave out, and he was sent hurdling through a sea of darkness. He landed on the murky floor and groaned, rolling to his side. Judging from the sharp pain ensuing with every breath, he was sure he had cracked or broken a few ribs.

He squinted, looking up as he tried to place where he had fallen from, but it was too dark to see his own fingertips. He reached into his pockets for his case of waterproof matches and cursed, realizing he must have left them near the opening of the cave.

"Can anybody hear me?" Thomas called out hesitantly.

A noise alerted him of another presence, and Thomas tensed, raising a hand to press against the cool stone that acted like a wall. He rose silently and followed the intriguing sound, taking care to stay near the rock wall. He was aware he was shaking but dismissed it as a shiver to warm himself, trying not to acknowledge his sudden fear. His hand met an empty gap, and he felt around it, surprised to find another, smaller hole.

Thomas knelt and crawled through, not sure what he was hoping to find. His discovery sent chills down his spine, and he staggered back, gasping in disbelief. He tried to run, but a sharp sting penetrated his skin, and he collapsed.

An odd feeling of serenity drifted over his senses, and Thomas smiled as he was pulled backward, vanishing into nothingness.

❊

Mark glanced down at the body he carefully carried. Night had quickly approached, and he shuddered, gazing at the moonlit beach. It was so much clearer here than in the city; he could actually see thousands of stars twinkling against the shady sky. Silvery light seemed to dance over the waters, and the sand reflected that hoary light into the air, creating a surreal feeling.

"Mark!" Mrs. Razat cried.

A small light was barely visible, but it was there, flickering in the distance. They hurried toward it, both gasping in surprise when they saw members of their family.

"Mom!" Mark cried and staggered forward. Once they reached the fire, Mark gently lowered Jason, carefully arranging his limbs into a more comfortable position.

"Mark!"

Mark was nearly knocked aside by a sturdy tackle, and he laughed, wrapping his arms around his younger sister.

"Marie! You're alive!" He glanced behind her and slumped in relief. "Will!"

William smiled bashfully and stepped closer to Mark and Marie. "Don't yell at me, Mark. I've had enough of arguments."

Mrs. Marcette hugged Mark tightly, and Mark gently wiped her tears away before hugging back.

"Mom!" Diego and Salatina chorused from their place by the fire.

Mrs. Razat laughed. "Oh, *mis niños!*" she cried, pulling them into a crushing hug.

"Rosetta."

Mrs. Razat released her children and spun around, clapping a hand to her mouth when she saw her husband.

"Carlos, *amor mío*! You're alive!" She grinned and jumped on him, dragging him to the sand. They rolled around playfully before she pulled him into a kiss.

"Ew! Mom!" Diego exclaimed and covered his sister's eyes.

Mrs. Marcette hurried over to Jason and began to warily inspect his injuries. After a while, she sat back on her heels and smiled. "He's going to be fine," she said. "It's better than it looks."

"That's a relief," Mrs. Razat said. She sat beside Jason and gently pushed his hair away from his sweaty skin. She glanced up at the moon and shuddered. "I hope the others are okay."

"Yes," said Mrs. Marcette. She sat across from the woman. "I hope so too."

❈

Another day had already passed, but now time had decided to be agonizingly slow as part of the group waited for their companions to return.

"How long are they going to take?" William asked, hugging his knees by the newly lit fire. "They've been gone all day." He poked the wood with a long stick and cringed when a cloud of embers erupted.

"Don't burn us," Jason muttered. He had woken up hours ago and now was clearly agitated that Julian was still missing.

"Hey!" someone shouted.

Jason's eyes widened. He looked around frantically. "That's Antonio!"

"Antonio?" Mrs. Marcette called out.

Four people quickly came into view; Julian was sandwiched between Mr. Marcette and Antonio, and Anitaa was quietly trailing behind. They all bared solemn expressions as they stumbled closer to the campsite.

"What happened?" asked Mrs. Marcette as Julian was lowered to the ground.

"Sandy's dead," said Antonio. "Julian found the body."

"Sandy's …?" Jason felt something hitch in his chest. He had known Sandy since grade school, and now he was … dead?

"It wasn't pretty," Antonio admitted. He looked a little green. "We found Julian near the body."

"We buried him," admitted Anitaa. Her face was streaked with tears and blood. "We couldn't leave him there to … to … to …"

Jason cut her off with a hug. She tensed for a moment before slumping against Jason. "Don't I get a hello kiss?" Mr. Marcette asked as he approached his wife, pulling her into a quick hug. Mrs. Marcette smiled and tilted her head into the curve of his shoulder. Mr. Marcette kissed her lightly. He smiled and turned to William and Marie.

"Don't reprimand me," William said quietly before Mr. Marcette could greet them. "I would jump again if I could; nothing changes. I'm just sorry I never said good-bye."

The fire beside them was dwindling. Mr. Razat took out a silver cylinder and extracted a few wooden sticks.

"Waterproof matches," he told Jason.

"On a scuba diving trip?"

"In case of emergencies," Mr. Razat responded. "And this turned out to be one."

"So, what exactly are we going to do?" William asked. "We can't sit around; we've got to do something!"

"Do what?" Antonio retorted. "No one knows we're here …"

"The hotel!" Diego's voice cut through Antonio's. "They know where we went! They'll send a search party! People will be here in no time!"

"If only we knew where here is," Salatina said.

"I'd guess out of all of us, Thomas would know," Mrs. Marcette said softly. She regarded the salty water that surrounded them with disdain, then turned her gaze to all the bloodied wounds around her. "Carlos, you didn't happen to bring a bowl with you?"

Mr. Razat shook his head.

"So that's it?" Anitaa muttered. "We're doing nothing?"

William gazed at the numerous distressed expressions and felt like crying. He forced himself to calm down and then glanced at Anitaa. "What else can we do?" he asked. Without waiting for an answer, he turned away and pretended to sleep.

※

The sun had begun its ascent into the sky a few hours earlier and now hung proudly amongst the fluffy clouds.

Julian sang quietly under his breath as he watched the waves crash against the shore and then reverse back into the ocean. The mist barely reached his face, but the salt in the air burned his open cuts.

"Early one morning, just as the sun was rising," he whispered softly as he let the light breeze caress his wild hair, "I heard a maid sing in the valley below." He let out a deep breath before shaking his head and closing his eyes. "Oh, don't deceive me, oh, never leave me." He blinked a few stray tears away. He frowned as he stuck a finger into the sand, turning the parched mixture, as red flakes of dried blood muddled in. "How could you use a poor maiden so?"

"You were always a sucker for the classics." Jason took a seat next to him. "But that one—you're always singing that one."

Julian flashed him a smile that never reached his eyes. "My mother used to sing it to me before she—it's one of the nice things I can remember."

Antonio joined the two silently.

"How's Anitaa?" Julian asked.

Antonio glanced behind him and frowned. "She's still crying, but Sandy *is* dead. You can't just snap and forget it all."

"Yes, I suppose not," Jason muttered and stood. "Grieve all you want; it's starting to look as if we have all the time in the world."

"We're back!" announced Mr. Razat. He appeared from the forest, and his hands were filled with fruits. "And we brought food."

"Did you find anything we could use as a bucket?" Mrs. Marcette asked indignantly.

Mr. Razat's face brightened. "Diego found some stuff that washed up on shore. Mark, your dad's back there waiting for you."

Mark jogged off, disappearing behind the large trees.

"Look what we found!" Salatina exclaimed at that moment, emerging from behind the trees. She dumped the pile of wet and broken items onto the sand.

"Ew," Diego muttered. He frowned as he did the same.

Salatina sent him an irked look and began rummaging through the pile. "We found a cup—it's bigger than a normal cup—is it all right, Mrs. Marcette?"

"It's fine," Mrs. Marcette said. "Who wants to be first?"

The leaves rustled slightly, and Mr. Marcette appeared in front of them, his expression filled with confusion.

"Michael?" Mrs. Marcette asked questionably.

"I thought you were sending Mark to help me?"

"I did. Didn't you see him?"

"No, did you?" No one answered. Mr. Marcette nervously chewed his lip and turned around. "Have any of you seen Mark?"

All he got in response were tentative shakes of heads and a few whispered nos.

7

"We split into groups of two, search for Mark, and then meet back here. Marie, you go with your mother. William, you're with me. As soon as it gets dark, I want everyone back here, no exceptions."

Jason grabbed Julian and pulled him into the forest.

"We should stay near the beach," said Julian. "We don't want to get lost."

"If Mark was on the beach, he wouldn't be missing."

Julian looked around. The trees towered, blocking out the few rays of sun. There were shadows that seeped from the roots, crawling over the ground and almost brushing against their feet.

"Mark? Are you here?" They waited but were doubtful of a response.

Julian clambered around the tree roots, holding the thick trunks for balance. "There's a cave over here." Julian peered into the dark cavern and shuddered.

"Julian, what's that? By your foot?"

There was something that looked like a chain half buried in the earth. Julian squatted and brushed the soil away, carefully pulling the chain into the air.

"It can't be," Jason said quietly. He quickly covered the short distance between him and Julian and stared hard at the object swinging back and forth. "Is it ... that *is* it, right?"

"I ... I think so," said Julian. "But, how?"

A twig snapped, and both boys swirled around, facing the bushes. Julian carefully placed the object in his pocket.

"Who's there?" Jason called out. "Mark?"

The bushes rattled for a moment before Salatina burst through, her face scruffy and covered with dirt.

"Thank god, I found someone!" she exclaimed and bounded toward them. "Diego ran away from me, the idiot." She looked around the area with interest. "Find anything interesting?"

"We were going to take a look inside that cave," said Jason.

Salatina followed them and then whistled in a high key. She squinted at something caught in the branches above them.

"Mark was wearing a green shirt, right?"

"Blue," both Julian and Jason corrected.

"A blue like that?"

Julian glanced up, noticing the strip of cloth that hung on one of the boughs.

Salatina walked closer to the cave and kicked a small box gently. She bent and retrieved it. "And look what else." She threw the box at Jason.

Jason fumbled slightly. "Quite the detective," he mumbled before he examined the small box.

"Are they Mark's?"

"Why would Mark carry waterproof matches?" Jason asked, as he slipped the box into his pocket. "I think they're Thomas's."

"Thomas? Wait, do you think they're together? In there?" Salatina asked.

"One way to find out." Jason crawled into the cave, disappearing into the clinging shadows.

Salatina smiled sweetly at Julian before motioning in front of her. "Age before beauty."

Julian followed Jason into the darkened hole. He heard Salatina behind him and shuddered, not liking the feeling of the dirt walls so close to him.

"Are you all right, Julian?"

"I'm not claustrophobic!"

"I never said you were."

"I'm not," Julian repeated weakly. A sudden cry surprised him, followed by a thick veil of silence. "Salatina?" Julian called out and listened carefully, trying not to panic.

"Wasn't me."

Julian began to tremble nervously. "Jason?" Silence was the only response, and dread began to creep through Julian's mind. "Jason!"

"Stop! Stop moving!"

"Jason ..."

A low groan interrupted Julian, and he stiffened as the ground below him gave way. With a yell, Julian plummeted into the darkness, landing on his back with a painful moan.

"Julian?"

Julian heard Salatina's frantic cries and tried to sit up. He listened as footsteps shuffled, and then the area was illuminated by a match Jason was holding.

"Salatina," Jason called out. "Where are you?"

A head popped out from a hole above them, and the boys saw Salatina's worried expression.

"Are you two ..."

"We're fine," Jason said quickly. "Get out of here and find help. *Quickly.*" Jason dropped the match when the flame brushed against his finger, and the cave was suddenly clouded by darkness.

"But ..."

"Now!"

Julian heard scrambling above. He rolled to his side and tried to say something, but the only sound that escaped him was a pathetic moan.

"Julian?"

Julian felt a hand grasp his back and push him to a sitting position.

"Are you okay?"

"Fine," Julian grunted.

"Is your thigh bleeding?"

Julian quickly checked. "No."

Jason struck another match, and they both shimmied backward until their backs pressed against the cave wall. They stared at the flickering flame; it was comforting to them both, providing them with a sense of security the darkness easily stripped away.

Jason sighed and closed his eyes before frowning. He cocked his head. "Do you hear that?"

"Yes," said Julian and then he paused. "It's ... footsteps?"

"Mark?" Jason whispered loudly. "Thomas? Is that ..."

"Jason!" Julian cried out suddenly as something wrenched Jason from his grasp. "J-Jason?" Julian stretched his arms in front of him.

A groan ensued to Julian's right, and he spun around. He had the vaguest feeling he was being watched somewhere in the shadows. His feet knocked against something behind him, and he tripped, crashing to the floor. Julian sat up with a low moan, crawling backward. His heart was racing.

"Julian?" Jason moaned.

Julian scrambled forward, groping the ground in an attempt to find Jason. A hand tightly grasped the back of his shirt, and Julian tensed.

"Jason?"

Instead of receiving an answer, Julian was slammed into the stone wall. His head hit the cold rock with brute force, and he groaned, slumping to the ground dazedly. He weakly felt the side of his head and pulled back when he found his fingers sticky. A hand wrapped around his neck and hauled him up roughly. His feet quickly left the ground, and he dangled in the air. His hands scratched in vain at the fingers wrapped around his neck. Julian kicked his legs blindly, his movements becoming more sluggish as time slowly trickled away. He was running out of air, and his attacker knew it.

8

"Julian," Jason whispered. He could hear Julian's cries grow weaker. He scrambled to his feet and rammed his body into the shady silhouette that was attacking Julian. He stumbled to the ground and groaned, planting a hand on his stomach. He pulled away at the stickiness and noticed from the pain that his wound had reopened.

Dazedly, Jason forced himself to his knees. He stretched his hands out and began to crawl forward, searching the cave floor for Julian's body. Jason's hands met with cold flesh, and he drew closer, grabbing the smaller wrist and desperately searching for a pulse.

"Thank god," he whispered in relief. He fumbled with his pocket before opening the tiny box and striking a match. A soft glow illuminated the cave, and Jason quickly scanned the area for any sight of their attacker. Flickering shadows seemed to be the only other thing present. Jason sighed, dropping the match to the stone floor and scooping Julian's limp body into his arms. Jason found the hole in the ceiling and laid Julian underneath, cursing as the light slowly died. He heard a soft thud to his right, and he paused. His hands slowly reached toward his pocket, but before he could grab the box of matches, he was tackled, and the matches were sent skidding across the cave floor.

A heavy body pinned him against the ground. Jason thrashed his limbs, planting a successful punch and hearing a definite crack. He scrambled past his attacker, his hands flailing as he tried to find the small box. His fingers finally curled around the object, and he pulled it to his chest, clambering backward until his back was pressed firmly against the wall. He fumbled to ignite the match and gasped in shock. The match fell from his fingers, landing with a soft thud against the hard floor.

"Mark?"

Mark was covered in soot. Scarlet scratches littered his face and hands, curling around his skin as though he had been grabbed by thorns. Mark's eyes were wide with fear, and his hands were shaking violently. He grabbed Jason's shirt with a balled-up fist and pulled him closer.

"You didn't bring anyone—no one came? No one ever comes—don't need them anyway."

Jason clenched Mark's hand, trying to pry his fingers from his shirt. He cringed when he noticed blood dripping from Mark's nose.

"Mark? That was you? You attacked us?"

"Attacked? No, defended." Mark's breathing became jagged, and Jason could make out his eyes darting from side to side. "I can't—I'm sorry. Go! Leave—run! Before it comes—comes back for us."

"What comes?" He tried not to flinch when Mark grabbed his shoulder.

"Water—can't eat, too hungry. Marie—where's my sister?"

Jason edged himself closer to the wall behind him. Mark made a sudden choking sound and collapsed on top of Jason, crushing the smaller teenager.

"Mark—" Jason strangled out. Mark remained silent. Jason finally rolled the teenager off of his chest and kicked his tangled limbs free. "Mark?" Jason crawled closer to the motionless teenager and shook him gently. "Mark?" Jason pressed two fingers to the side of Mark's neck and gasped, finding no pulse.

Jason hastily struck another match and froze. Mark's eyes were open, staring blankly at the cavern ceiling. A small pool of crimson was slowly forming under his head, coating the floor. Jason scrambled back and instantly searched the cave.

"Jason?"

Jason's head snapped up. Antonio's head was peeping from the hole in the cavern ceiling.

"Is that Mark?"

Jason ignored Antonio's horrified tone. "We have to get out of here!"

"It's Mark, isn't it?"

"Antonio, we ..."

"Is Mark ..."

"He's dead! He's dead, and whatever killed him is in this cave!"

Antonio nodded shakily. Jason grabbed Julian, easily lifting the light teenager into the air.

Antonio leaned forward and made a swipe for Julian's limp body.

"Okay," said Antonio, "I got him."

Jason watched blurrily as Julian disappeared through the hole in the ceiling. He rubbed his arms nervously and glanced around the hollow cavern, his eyes slowly settling on Mark's prone body—or where Mark's body was laying just minutes ago; only a trail of fresh blood remained.

"Antonio? Antonio!"

"Don't worry," said Antonio, reappearing once more. "I'm not going anywhere. What about Mark?"

"He's gone!"

"I just saw him!"

Jason was shaking now. "Something took him! There's something in this cave!"

Antonio nodded and lowered his arms. Jason took a running leap and managed to hook his fingers around Antonio's hands. He was slowly hoisted through the dark shadows. Jason felt a sudden lurch, and he tightened his grip, squeezing his eyes shut.

"Don't worry; I've got you," said Antonio, and soon Jason was pulled into the small tunnel above the hollow cave.

Dazed, Jason followed Antonio out of the narrow burrow. His eyes burned when he saw the bright light ahead. He crawled out of the channel and swayed. His head began to throb, and the light hurt his eyes so much that they watered. He struggled to stand and then crumbled limply to the ground.

❊

Antonio ran a hand through his mangled hair. "We can't tell them."

"Are you kidding? If what you said is true …"

"Of course it's true. I saw him with my own eyes."

"I just can't believe he's dead," said Salatina. "He was alive a few days ago, and now he's not."

"Yes," said Antonio. "Just like how he was lying there one minute, and then the next he's gone. How can we explain that to anyone? I wouldn't believe it myself if I hadn't seen it."

"And why aren't we going to tell anyone?"

Antonio glanced around carefully before lowering his voice to a whisper. "Do you really want to be the one to tell the Marcettes that Mark is *dead*?"

"We can't just lie to them," exclaimed Anitaa.

Antonio sighed wearily. "You guys didn't see Jason down there. He was *scared*. And I mean really, really scared. I've known Jason for a long time, and Jason doesn't get scared. He gets annoyed, and he gets angry, and he gets agitated, but he *never* gets scared."

"So we keep it a secret?" Salatina asked guiltily.

"We just don't talk about it."

❈

Julian gingerly held his throat before opening his mouth. Like last time, his voice came out in a raspy whisper. He crossed his arms, and his shoulders slumped in defeat. He crawled over to Jason and tugged Jason's arm, attempting to wake him up.

"Julian, let him sleep."

Jason groaned unconsciously and began to stir. He attempted to turn himself over and then just sighed sleepily.

"Diego," Mrs. Marcette said softly, "bring me some of the boiled water." She turned back to Jason and smiled as his lashes began to flutter.

Diego carefully handed the chipped cup to her. They watched as Jason's eyes opened, and he bolted upright.

"Julian!" he exclaimed, looking around frantically before his eyes settled on Julian. Without warning, Jason launched himself at the teenager, knocking them both to the sand. "You're alive!"

Julian hugged his friend back, flustered at Jason's sudden reaction. He held his throat softly and then shook his head.

Mrs. Marcette handed Jason the water and rubbed his back as he drank the cooling liquid. "Anywhere else hurt?"

"I think I'm okay," he muttered. "Can I walk around for a bit? Stretch my legs?"

"I guess so," Mrs. Marcette said slowly.

Antonio and Anitaa helped the two to their feet, and then the four slowly made their way toward the sandy rocks by the ocean. They sat wearily and stayed silent for a long moment.

"No one else knows?" Jason asked.

Antonio shook his head. "Just us and Sal. But that doesn't mean they're not going to ask. What will we tell them?"

"The truth."

"The truth?" Anitaa repeated. "The truth sounds like a lie."

"We're only telling the adults," said Jason. "I don't want Marie or William to hear it from us; I want them to hear it from family." He paused, eyes glazed over. "It's always easier that way."

"When?"

"Tonight."

❋

"Is there a reason we're here and not asleep?" Mr. Marcette yawned loudly as if to emphasize his point.

"Yes," said Jason. "But first, we have something to show you."

Mr. Razat gasped when Julian removed an object from his pocket. He stepped closer to Julian and froze, eyes widening slightly.

"Is that what I think it is?" Mr. Razat held his hand toward the object, and Julian delicately passed it to the man. Mr. Razat raised his hand to the moonlight, eyes glistening as the trinket glittered.

"Why is a rusted necklace so important?" Mr. Marcette asked.

Immediately a look of offense crossed the trio's expressions. Mr. Razat held it up, and Jason noted the way their eyes unconsciously followed its path.

"Sapphires, rubies, diamonds, and emeralds," Jason said softly, gesturing to the dirty string of beads at the front. "Custom-made for Jessica Monroe, a gift from her husband, Arthur. They were explorers in the 1700s, but they vanished—quite literally—without a trace."

"I remember this story," Mr. Razat said. "The Monroes were researching a different kind of plant, one that consumed meat as its main food source. Their research led them to believe a specific island in the Philippines accommodated the type of plant they were looking for."

"They took off in a sailboat with a promise to be back in a month," continued Jason. "The first month passed without any contact from them, and then another month, and then another. After three months, a search party was sent out, but they found nothing—not their boat, not their bodies, not even the island the Monroes had set out to find."

Julian slipped the necklace into his pocket.

"But that would mean this island …"

"Was the one they were looking for," finished Jason.

"We don't know if they were actually here," said Mrs. Razat. "The necklace could have washed up on shore; it doesn't prove anything."

"It was nowhere near the shore."

"An animal could've carried it," protested Mrs. Marcette.

"Have you seen any? Any birds? Any fish? Have you seen any living thing here besides us and plants?"

"What are you getting at?" Mr. Marcette said finally. He didn't waver at the glare Jason shot him.

"They made it here, Jessica and Arthur. They either made it safely or crashed like us, but they still made it here …"

"And they never left," Julian added quietly.

"There's something else," said Jason. "It's about Mark."

9

"You saw Mark?" Mrs. Marcette asked finally. She seemed paler, the dark rings around her eyes more prominent in the moonlight.

"He was the one who did this to us," Jason said.

"No!" Mr. Marcette exclaimed. "Liar! Mark would never ..."

"Where is he?" Mrs. Marcette demanded.

Julian exchanged a miserable look with Jason.

Jason cleared his throat softly. "He's dead."

Mr. Marcette grabbed Jason's shirt and slammed him against the tree trunk. Julian winced as Jason's head thudded against bark.

"I dare you to repeat that!"

"Michael!"

Mr. Marcette released his hold and allowed Mrs. Marcette to pull him back.

"Mark wasn't himself," said Jason. He was staring at the ground instead of the Marcettes. "He kept muttering things that made no sense." He raised his head. "He tried to kill Julian and would have succeeded if I hadn't stopped him!"

"You're lying!"

"I wish I was," Jason admitted. "Mark was talking nonsense, and then he just fell."

"He fell?" Mr. Marcette repeated in disbelief. He laughed, but it wasn't a happy sound. "He just fell? Did you hear that, Lynn? Our son *fell*."

"Stop it, Michael," Mrs. Marcette chided quietly. "What do you mean *fell?*"

"He just collapsed. He wasn't breathing; he had no pulse."

"And you just left his body?" Mrs. Marcette cried. "You left his body to rot?"

Julian made a choking noise in his throat.

"I had to choose between a dead body and a live one."

"You could have taken both!" exclaimed Mr. Marcette.

"You weren't down there!"

"Arguing is not going to change the fact that Mark *is* dead," Julian interrupted. He almost stepped back at the intense stare he received.

"He's right," admitted Mrs. Marcette. Her shoulders began to shake as she fidgeted with her hands. "Mark's dead!"

Mr. Marcette tried to wrap his arms around her, but she pushed him away and turned to Rosetta.

"I just wish it wasn't like this," Julian murmured to Jason. "When did things get so horrible?"

"When are things not?" Jason countered. "We're just going to have to deal with it."

❈

"Dad?" William asked in confusion, as he watched his parents stumble toward them. They were yelling at each other. William rubbed his eyes as he sat up. "What's going on?"

"Go back to sleep," Mr. Marcette snapped.

"Daddy?" Marie repeated. "Did something happen?"

"I said go to sleep!"

Marie jumped and dug her fingers into William. William winced but did nothing to stop her.

Mrs. Marcette broke into a dry, hacking sob. She slumped to the cold sand and buried her face in her quivering hands.

"Mom?" William asked quietly. "Dad? What's going on?"

"I can't take this anymore!" Mrs. Marcette exclaimed. "Michael, I can't do this! My son is gone! He's just ..."

"Mark?" asked William hopefully. "You've found Mark?"

"Don't use that as an excuse!" Mr. Marcette growled, ignoring William's question.

Mrs. Marcette staggered back at the accusation, a hand seizing at her heart. "An excuse? *An excuse?* Michael, my child is *dead*!"

"Mark's *what*?" Marie exclaimed. Her eyes never left her parents. "Will, Mark's *what*?"

"They're lying," William whispered back. "It's all a joke; it has to be."

William watched their father lean toward their mother and mutter something before she sent him staggering with a furious slap.

"It doesn't seem like a joke," Marie whispered. "Mom?" She sniffed. "Dad?"

William followed their parents with his eyes as they both stamped into the forest, still arguing and oblivious to their children.

❁

"Carlos, stop pacing," said Mrs. Razat in a weary, monotone voice. "You are giving me a headache."

"If you don't want to see me pace, then don't look," snapped Mr. Razat. Immediately, his visage softened. "I'm sorry, Rosetta," he said quietly. "I don't mean that."

"Of course you did."

"This is not my fault," Mr. Razat said quietly.

"I never said it was," answered Mrs. Razat, but something in her expression defied her words.

"I did nothing wrong!"

"What are you saying? This is my fault? That I deserve this?"

"*I* thought this vacation was a bad idea. *You* were the one who wanted to go. I was perfectly fine …"

"You were fine locked up in your office, drooling over your work! If I hadn't pushed you, you would have never left! That's all you ever do—work! You barely come home anymore!"

"My work is what pays for the family. It's why we have a house; it's why we're not starving every day!"

Mrs. Razat glanced up at her husband and then shook her head, defeated. "I'm finished," she said quietly.

"Finished?"

"I'm done with this, Carlos." She choked back a sob and shook her head. "I can't live like this any longer."

"You're quitting? Rosetta, we've been married for nineteen years!"

"Exactly!" Mrs. Razat cried. "For nineteen years, I've put up with the fact that your work is number one, and we're number two! I'm losing my love for you, Carlos, and I don't know what else to do!" She turned around and dashed into the thick woods, unable to face her husband any longer. She ignored the cries behind her as she ran.

❋

"Have you found her yet?"
Mr. Razat shook his head, not meeting Jason's stare.
"I'm sure she just got lost."
Mr. Razat glanced over his shoulder, staring at the grisly forest.
"The others are still searching." When Jason still received no answer, he left Mr. Razat and joined Julian on the sand.
"Everything that could go wrong is happening." Jason sighed and glanced at Julian. He was staring at Antonio with his eyebrows furrowed together.
"Does he seem a bit off to you?"
"I don't see anything different," muttered Jason.
"Look at where he's staring."
Jason followed Antonio's gaze to Anitaa. "I can see what he's staring at, but that isn't unusual, now is it? He's had a crush on her since the day they met."
"No, look at the *way* he's looking at her."
Jason could clearly see the jealousy as it danced across Antonio's intense expression. "He better not try anything," he said in a low voice. "This place seems to be making people do the stupidest of things. It's like they can't think logically anymore."
"It's because they're scared," Julian said.
"Aren't we all?"

❋

Marie looked up when she saw a shadow fall over her and William. She saw her mother looming over them. Mrs. Marcette's eyes were rimmed red, her face splotchy and covered in tears.
"What do you want?" William muttered.
Marie winced when his grip tightened on her arm.
"Just to talk," Mrs. Marcette whispered. She sounded broken.
"And Dad?"
"If he wants to join us," she said, lacking enthusiasm.
Marie knew her parents had fought but couldn't understand the hate in her mother's voice when she spoke of their father. Marie caught her father's eye and shyly motioned him over.

Mr. Marcette joined the trio on the sand. He sat tensely between William and Mrs. Marcette. "What do you want?"

"What do I want?" repeated William. "Aren't you going to tell us what happened?"

"Mark's dead. Julian and Jason found him in a cave."

Marie winced at the blunt tone and had to force herself not to cry out. She glanced at William. His hands were clenched into fists, and he was shaking.

"We know that," he growled and jerked his thumb backward. "They told us after you two ran off." William scoffed and made a point of observing them with a frown. "And you call yourselves parents."

"Damn it!" Mr. Marcette snapped. He rose to his feet. "Don't you dare, William! You don't talk to us like that. We're your parents."

William mirrored Mr. Marcette's stance. His body language was oozing with defiance. "Parents?" he jeered and laughed mockingly. "Some parents. You can't even hold on to your child …"

Marie shrieked in surprise when her father tackled William to the ground.

"Michael!" Mrs. Marcette cried.

It took Mr. Razat, Antonio, and Jason to drag the livid man off of William, but eventually they were able to restrain him.

William stood on shaky legs with Julian's help. He wiped his lip and winced at the crimson that stained his pale wrist.

Mr. Marcette's eyes widened at the sight of blood. "Will," he murmured and took a step toward his son.

William scrambled back in alarm. "Don't." He held his hands out, palms facing his father. "Don't say it because you sure as hell don't mean you're sorry."

Marie trembled slightly before stepping closer to her father. "Dad," she said softly. "Can I ask you something?"

Mr. Marcette gulped shakily but nodded. He breathed deeply as if trying to compose himself.

Marie paused to look her father's heaving body over, taking in the red-stained nails, the bloodied knuckles, and the lack of wounds on his part. "When did my father become such a monster?"

※

Antonio grabbed Anitaa's wrist and pulled her away from everyone else. "Anitaa," he whispered in her ear, "I need to tell you something." His eyes were wide, his pupils enlarged, and his breathing hectic.

Anitaa pulled away from Antonio and stood closer to Jason.

"Anitaa, you and I have something …"

"Nothing," Anitaa interrupted. "We have nothing, Antonio."

Antonio shook his head and tried to pull her closer. "Anitaa, please! I love …"

"Don't say it," Anitaa cried. "You don't love me, Antonio! You had your chance and you ruined it."

Jason clutched Antonio's shoulder and drew him away. Antonio tried to shrug off the strong grip.

"Run away with me, Anitaa. As soon as we get off this island, we can get married …"

"You don't understand," Anitaa said seriously. "I don't love you! You're just a friend, nothing more and nothing less."

Antonio glared at Anitaa and spun around, delivering a solid punch to Jason. Jason stumbled and clutched his nose, grunting in pain. Antonio smirked before turning back. His smile faded when his eyes settled on Julian instead of Anitaa.

"Where'd she go?"

Julian ignored his question.

"Anitaa, sooner or later you'll have to accept it!" he shouted instead. "I love you, and you may not know it yet, but you love me too!" Antonio glanced at Julian before running forward and swinging his arms wildly.

Julian dodged the punches with an oddly familiar ease. "Antonio, stop this," he exclaimed, as he barely ducked in time to avoid a messy kick at his face.

"Stay out of this," Antonio warned, panting. He charged at Julian.

Julian elegantly whirled Antonio around and placed his arms around Antonio's head, applying a small amount of pressure. Antonio struggled in Julian's arms before his flailing limbs slowly stilled, and he drifted into a world of unconsciousness.

10

Jason propped Antonio's body against one of the trees, using his other hand to stop the small flow of blood. Anitaa hurried out of the forest and ran to Jason's side.

"It's fine," protested Jason. "He didn't break it." He would never admit it, but his nose was hurting like hell. He just knew the skin over the bone was going to be bruised blue by tomorrow.

"I don't know what happened!" Anitaa exclaimed. "He just …"

"He's probably delirious," suggested Julian. "We hardly have anything nutritious to eat, and the heat is unbearable. Things happen."

Anitaa pulled the two teenagers into a trembling embrace. "Let's just … Will he be okay here?"

"Nothing's going to get him," said Jason.

Julian nodded and cringed when Jason elbowed him softly.

"Nice move back there." Jason's expression changed when he noticed Julian's sobered look. "Your father?"

Anitaa quickly intervened, taking Julian's hand and pulling him behind her. "Well stop thinking about him; he doesn't deserve it."

Jason slung an arm around Julian's shoulder and pulled him closer. "Julian, he's dead and gone. You need to forget about him." Jason caught Anitaa's eye and she nodded, leaving the two teenagers. Jason faced Julian, using his clean hand to pull Julian to the sand. They waited in silence for more than a few minutes, not sure how to begin the conversation.

"I can't forget him," Julian said quietly, bringing his knees to his chest. "Not now, not ever."

"Then stop thinking about him."

"Can we talk about something else?" Julian asked in a meek tone.

Jason smiled and stretched out on his back. "Remember the time Jesse decided I needed a makeover?"

"You're a good brother to him," Julian said as he closed his eyes. They fluttered open immediately when he felt Jason's hand on his shoulder.

"You're a good brother to me."

"*Adoptive* brother," Julian corrected. "It's not the same thing."

Jason grinned. "To me it is."

※

Jason awoke when he felt someone shaking his shoulder gently. He yawned and blinked, trying to get used to the bright light that surrounded him.

"Anitaa?" he asked when he noticed her kneeling next to him. She looked worried.

"Antonio didn't come back."

Jason raised an eyebrow at Anitaa's statement, puzzled by her anxious tone.

"Don't tell me you're not worried!" she exclaimed. "He could be in trouble!"

"What trouble? He's probably too embarrassed to face us. I bet he's wallowing in self-pity this very moment."

"I'm still worried, and I'll go look for him with or without you." Anitaa's lip trembled as she looked up at Jason, eyes faintly wet with unshed tears. "I just thought I'd be safer with you."

"Fine," Jason muttered.

He hooked his arm around Anitaa's and pulled her toward the forest, seeking out the tall tree he had laid Antonio under. His eyes widened, and he heard Anitaa gasp. Her body stiffened beside him.

"Get someone," he said as he quivered. His voice cracked. He heard Anitaa run back and closed his eyes. He tried to calm himself with deep breaths. He took a step back, turning around and fixing his gaze on the waves that crashed onto the shore.

"Jason?" he heard Mr. Razat exclaim.

"Jason, what is it?" Julian asked as he jogged closer and then stopped. Jason heard a sharp intake of breath. "Tell me that's not blood …"

"What happened?" Mr. Razat demanded. "Who did this?"

Jason ignored the man and grabbed Julian's hand, dragging him away from the bloodied sand.

"Is it true?" Marie asked as soon as they reached the crowd.

"He's not dead," Julian insisted. He yanked his hand from Jason and clutched it to his chest. "He's not dead! He's just injured … right?"

Jason could almost feel the intensity of Julian's stare. He didn't know what to say.

"He's not!" Julian repeated. "Right? Right?"

No one answered.

❂

Marie clutched Diego's sleeve, terrified by the eerie silence that greeted them in the shady forest. She glanced around. The branches were waving at them from above though there was little wind present.

"I don't think this was our best idea," Marie whispered to Salatina. "This place doesn't seem right; there's something about it that's … off."

Salatina nodded. Her hand was clutching Diego's other arm as they roamed farther into the woods.

"Don't worry," Diego advised breezily. "We'll be out of here in no time. All we need to do is pick some more fruits for everyone and then get them back together—and this part is the easiest."

Marie nibbled on her lower lip. Her eyes darted from tree to tree as the trunks creaked and groaned in the soil below. "And why did we tell no one where we were going?"

"Because we wanted them to be surprised?" Diego said, but it sounded as if he were guessing. "Anyone else get that feeling something really bad is about to happen?"

"Let's just forget about the fruits and get out of here," Salatina said. "I don't like this anymore."

Diego wiggled his arms from the girls' solid grips and rested his hands on his hips. "Which way is out?"

Neither girl answered.

Diego wrapped his arms around his waist as he bounced on the balls of his feet. "So we're stuck here?"

"We'll just walk one way until we reach the beach."

"That, or we can scream," suggested Marie, leaning toward the second option. She opened her mouth to do so but jumped back when Salatina pressed her hand against her lips. Marie mumbled something against the rough palm before pushing it away.

"If they find us they'll never trust us again!" Salatina exclaimed.

"Fine, we won't scream," Marie agreed, "but I'm not walking around for hours either. I want to get out of here and fast." Marie turned to Diego, surprised to see he wasn't beside her anymore. "Salatina, where's your brother?"

Salatina turned in a circle. "Diego?"

"He couldn't have gone far," Marie assured her.

Salatina sized up a large tree before taking a step back and leaping toward it.

"What are you doing?"

Salatina reached for a higher branch and easily pulled herself onto the cracked limb. "Trying to find my brother." She secured her footing before peering over the flourishing leaves. She wrinkled her forehead, pointing to a spot not too far from Marie. "I see something," she exclaimed, gesturing to the tracks in the dirt.

"Sal?" Marie said as she traced the pattern in the soil. Marie looked up with a worried expression. "These look like drag marks."

Salatina dropped from her perch. Gently, she reached out with two fingers and smoothed the soil away. "I don't understand," she whispered. She pushed her hair back and rubbed her eyes with the pale end of her wrist. "He couldn't have just disappeared."

Marie stared at the unusual tracks. Her eyes were glued to the dirt in front of her. Leaves and twigs caught her attention along the pathway, but the dotted blood beside them was what *held* her attention.

"Something's wrong," Marie whispered, squatting closer to the ground. "Why would he be bleeding?" Marie dabbed the liquid carefully and brought her fingers closer to her face, rubbing the blood over her fingers in fascination. "Since we've been here, we haven't seen any animals. This blood *has* to be Diego's." Marie's eyebrows dropped, curving toward her eyes. She spun around, a hand on the ground to keep her balance as she searched the air that faced her. She looked back to the ground, only to find another set of tracks, this time fresh and layered with more blood. Marie staggered back in fear, clutching her arms as she backed into a tree.

"Salatina?"

Something against Maria's ankle twitched, and Marie jumped, falling as she became entangled with the roots around her. She crawled backward, her eyes widening as they settled on the spiked vine in front of her. Its point was trembling slightly.

Marie closed her eyes, curling herself into a tight ball. "It's just the wind," she said, but she couldn't help when a scream surfaced from her lips.

❈

William's head jerked when he heard a screech come from somewhere deep within the woods. His piercing eyes narrowed as they entered the forest. He twisted his neck slightly.

"That was Marie," he exclaimed, tightening his grip on the sharp stick he clutched closely. "If she's in trouble ..."

"We will find her and help her. End of story," Jason interrupted. "This is no one's fault but theirs. They went in without telling us."

William took the lead, worry fueling his motions. "What were they thinking?" he muttered. "I'm going that way." William nodded his head farther north.

"We're not splitting up."

"Scared something might get me?" William taunted, leaning his shoulder against a neighboring tree. "There's nothing here that can kill, so relax."

"You don't understand," cried Jason. "There are dangerous things here!"

"No, you don't understand!" William exclaimed, pushing away from his stance. "There's *nothing* here! How many birds have flown over us? How many bugs have you swatted? How many animal cries have you heard? None. Zero. Zilch. Nada. Nothing! Truth is, Jason, there is nothing on this island except for vegetation and us. And I'm not scared of either. I don't care what you say; I'm going to find my little sister."

"And what if we can't find you?"

William froze before slowly turning to face Jason.

"What if whatever happened to Thomas ..."

"Thomas died. Drowned."

"And Antonio? I know you went to look, and I know you saw all the blood. He didn't drown, William."

"Whatever did that to Antonio could be doing that to my sister," William said softly.

Mr. Marcette pushed past, eyeing the teenagers with annoyance. "Stop arguing and start looking."

"I think I hear something," Mr. Razat said softly. He walked to the right and parted the bushes before gasping. He vanished from sight, leaving the others in confusion.

William quickly followed. "Marie!" he cried. He ran forward and ducked under the low branch. He knelt beside her, and she curled tighter into her body. He gently brushed stray strands of hair from Marie's grim face and rubbed her arms soothingly. "What happened?"

Marie sniffed and pulled Diego's limp body closer.

"Marie?" Mr. Marcette asked in surprise. His voice seemed softer.

"Diego?" Mr. Razat whispered.

"Marie, what happened?" William asked again. His eyes pleaded for an answer.

"Salatina," she whispered. Fresh tears coated her cheeks.

"Salatina?" asked Mr. Razat quietly. "Where is she?"

"Dead."

❄

Jason paced relentlessly in the sand, kicking up the dirt. Beyond him sat Julian, who was watching Jason with a bored expression. His dark hair whipped around his head as the wind picked up, sending tremors down his spine. Julian fixed his stare at the Marcettes, amazed to see that they were together and not arguing for once. They were all gathered around the unconscious duo, worry seeping through their motions.

"He's been going for a while," Anitaa whispered from beside Julian, mirroring his posture.

Julian's eyes flickered to his left before returning to Jason. "It's Jason," he said as if that explained everything. And it did.

Anitaa tugged her hair over one shoulder and began to braid the dirty locks. Julian watched from the corner of his eyes as Anitaa weaved the strands in and out, never pausing until she came to the end. She frowned before abandoning the hair, and a quarter of it twisted free from the braid.

"Aren't you the least bit curious?"

Julian nibbled on his chewed lip silently, wincing as he unintentionally drew blood. "Of course," he said, raising his hand to his lip and then setting it down when he realized it was covered in dirt. "But I'm not impatient. I can wait."

Anitaa glanced at her filth-covered hands and placed them on her braid, smoothing the hair. They stayed in silence for a longer moment before Anitaa rubbed her forearms. "I lost my chance."

Julian watched her lower her eyes.

"If it had been anywhere else, at a different time, I think I would've said yes. I was scared because he hurt me before. It took me so long to realize he wasn't ready to commit, and then I had to work so hard to pretend everything about us was normal. And suddenly he wants to change that? What else was

I supposed to say? I still do though, and—despite everything—I don't think I ever stopped."

"Love," Julian said with a sigh. "It's a weird, crazy, *unforgettable* thing that has us on the edge of our seats. It's confusing, isn't it? It makes you feel like a little kid again, all giddy and excited. But it's impossible to ignore, to pretend it's not there. Anitaa, you loved him like I love you and Jason. But did you *love* him?"

"Like you love her?" Anitaa asked, tilting her head toward the Marcettes.

Julian sighed forlornly. "Am I that obvious?"

"The way you look at her, the way your eyes sparkle. How you fiddle with your clothes whenever she's near and try not to stare at her eyes that seem to match yours *perfectly*. She feels the same way."

"Do you think so?"

"Of course," Anitaa said.

Julian hugged her and pulled her closer. "But you did love him," he said rather than asked, wiping her tears as they wet her cheeks.

"I hate it," she whispered. "I hate feeling like this—like … like something inside is broken, and I can't fix it, no matter how hard I try. No matter how much I want to, I can't feel whole anymore. I'm empty, Julian. I'm drained to a point where nothing else matters—where feelings are a thing of the past, and hope and love are bare and bleak." Anitaa sighed. "I'm a terrible person."

"You're not a terrible person," Julian argued. "You didn't know this would happen; none of us did."

"I killed him!" Anitaa exclaimed. "I stabbed him in the heart! I hurt him where it hurts the most."

"Anitaa," protested Julian, "that's not true. You can't change how you felt—you can't change how you *feel*. Why do you think love is so confusing? It gets its kicks by watching people like us try to understand it. People like you and me—we have to stand strong, offer no resistance, and refuse to back down when it comes to love. We can never give up on it because it's a part of us, no matter how broken up inside we are."

Anitaa hugged Julian, burying her face into the curve of his shoulder. "I'm so lucky to have a friend like you."

"I'll always be your friend," Julian informed Anitaa, his tone full of the overwhelming sincerity he was known for. He smiled. "No matter what." His palm faced her, waiting until she was ready. Anitaa planted her palm against Julian's and spread their fingers before crossing the digits.

"No matter what."

❊

Marie groaned pathetically when she felt a pounding in her head. She opened her eyes and had to blink away the blurriness.

"Marie!" William cried, and Marie felt arms wrap tightly around her body. "You have no idea how much you scared me!"

"Will?" Marie asked. She pushed him away. Her eyebrows furrowed in confusion as she stared at her new cuts and scrapes.

Beside her, someone moaned miserably. She glanced to the side in time to see Diego sit up, pressing a hand against his forehead.

"What happened?" he asked groggily.

"We were hoping you could tell us," Mr. Marcette said.

"Oh, right," he muttered and then shook his head. "Where's Salatina?"

Marie tensed in fear. Diego seemed to sense Marie's apprehension because he began to panic, looking around frantically. "Salatina," he repeated more urgently, struggling to stand. "Where is she?" Diego glanced at Marie's quivering body and lunged for her. "Where is she? Where's my sister?"

Marie scrambled back, choking out a muffled response.

Diego froze. "Say that again," he demanded.

"She's dead," Marie repeated miserably. William hugged her again, and Marie pulled him closer. "You disappeared, and then so did Salatina. There was a trail, and I followed it, but I couldn't see. It was dark. Something grabbed my ankle and pulled." Marie shuddered, remembering the horrible feeling.

"What about my sister?"

Marie pressed herself closer to William. "I was so sure ... so sure she was alive. She was against a tree, staring. Her eyes wouldn't follow me. She'd just stare past. I tried to wake her! I tried so hard, but she wouldn't move; she wouldn't blink." Marie met Diego's eyes. "And I turned to see if I could find you, and when I looked back she was gone. You were near the edge of a cave. I dragged you as far as I could, and then I heard the voices."

Julian wrinkled his forehead. "There's one more thing that I can't wrap my finger around," he said.

"Julian," warned Jason, "not now."

"This is important." He nibbled on his lip. "Did you see what did this to you?"

Marie shook her head.

"I remember."

She turned to Diego.

He was trembling. "I remember," he repeated. "*It* dragged me away just like that, like I was nothing. *It* took me away from you and," his voice cracked, "Sal, and then I went numb. I could hear you call my name, and I could see you two searching, but I could do nothing except watch. I couldn't move or speak." Diego raised his arms, and Marie flinched at the sight of the red-tinted dots that covered his skin. "I was pulled into a dark hole, and everywhere I looked I saw bones."

"Who did this?" Mr. Marcette asked. He was cracking his knuckles.

Diego scuffed. "Not who—far from who. *It. It* did this. *It* killed them all. I would have never believed it if I hadn't seen it with my own eyes. It shouldn't be real, but it is. Real enough to hurt, to bruise—*to kill*. And no one's going to believe me."

"Diego," Mr. Razat said, as he rubbed his son's back, "there's nothing to be afraid of; you can tell us."

"You'll all think I'm crazy. *I* think I'm crazy, but … it explains everything. It makes sense."

"Diego?"

Diego shuddered and stared at the sand. "*It's* like a gigantic Venus Fly Trap, but with one exception. Instead of bugs, *it* eats people."

11

"You can't be serious." Mr. Marcette was the first to sneer. "Plants *eating* people? Plants can't even eat meat!"

"There are plants that eat insects," Anitaa informed him in a quiet voice.

"Those are *insects*."

Mrs. Marcette nodded shakily. "Maybe it was ... I don't know; maybe it was Thomas?"

"Thomas couldn't do that. He's dead," argued William.

"Do you have any proof?" asked Mrs. Marcette. "We found no bodies."

"We don't need any proof! Diego saw ..."

"Diego doesn't know what he saw!" Mr. Marcette snapped. "Diego was traumatized. He just imagined Thomas was a plant ..."

"I'm not traumatized, and I didn't see Thomas!" Diego protested.

"It's impossible!" Mrs. Marcette exclaimed. "A plant cannot eat something as large as a human. It wouldn't be able to digest all the meat, the tissues, the organs, the bones."

"Dad," Diego said and shook his father's shoulder. "You know I'm right. And *I* know you've studied plant mutations. They'll believe you, Dad. Just explain, please!"

Mr. Razat barely nodded. "It's certainly not impossible," he said weakly. "Very unlikely, but not impossible. Meat-eating plants have a slight nature of evolving in a unique way that many other plants fail to do. Organisms that mutate faster than they should tend to mess up their genetic strands. The more they mutate, the faster they climb the steps up the evolutionary scale. It's possible that a plant that feeds on food as large as a human has evolved and exists. Of course, they would have to eat other meat to survive …"

"And that explains why there are no animals here! No birds, no insects, no fish! Nothing!" William exclaimed, cutting off Mr. Razat.

Mr. Razat nodded. "And it wouldn't hurt to have some sort of chemical synthesis to thrive off when food is scarce. If they had vines that were strong enough they could use them like hands, or if they were long enough they could stretch overseas in search of food!"

"The marks on our legs," Julian whispered in awe. "It brought us here to …"

"It's not logical," Mr. Marcette muttered. He shook his head in disbelief.

"A brilliant scientist once told me that evolution works in unusual ways, and logic doesn't have to be one of them," Mr. Razat informed him.

"I think it would be best if we all got some sleep," Jason said, staring at the tired faces around him.

Immediately, William stiffened. "You think I'm going to sleep after this? Sleep when that *thing* is out there?"

"Stop being melodramatic," Marie said softly. "We're not stupid; some will sleep, and some will stay awake. After a few hours, we can switch."

"I'm not melodramatic," William muttered, blood rushing to his face when he heard a number of snorts follow his comment.

Mrs. Marcette smiled. "William, you're the exact *definition* of melodramatic."

Anitaa sighed and gazed at the forest. It looked darker, more dangerous than before. "Who's going to take the first shift? How are we going to decide?"

Julian glanced around the beach, and he hesitantly approached one of the trees that sat on the edge of the forest. He broke a thin twig from a branch and then snapped the twig into nine pieces. "Choose one," he said, "and the two with the shortest sticks get to stay awake first."

❃

"Color?" Marie asked as she fiddled with the end of a stick in front of her.

Jason reached out with a thick stub of a branch and stirred the ashes, raising the fire from its wooden tomb. "Blue," he answered, not giving the onslaught of questions much thought; the answers seemed to come easier that way.

"Green," Marie responded, though he never asked. "Book?"

"*Hamlet.*"

"*The Little Princess.* Hobby?"

"I don't have one," Jason lied.

Marie sighed loudly and threw the stick into the fire. "Why us? I keep thinking this is all a dream—or worse, a nightmare. Mark's dead; Mom and Dad are fighting; William hates them both; Julian loves Anitaa; and there's a plant out to eat us!"

Jason frowned. "What did you say?"

Marie shrugged, but Jason wasn't fooled by her nonchalant act.

"I said there's a plant ready to devour our ... "

"Before that."

"Julian loves Anitaa," she spat out. "They're always together, always all over each other."

"Marie, you're an idiot." He smiled when he saw the stunned expression on her face.

"*Excuse me?*"

"I said you're an idiot. Julian is head over heels in love with you; it's written across his face clear as rain. Julian and Anitaa—they're just really good friends."

"He loves me?" Marie repeated softly. A smile slowly formed on her lips. She shook her head, and then a hesitant expression flitted across her face. "What about Antonio and Sandy? Were you close to them?"

Jason thought about his late friend and chuckled. "Sandy and I had a ... an odd relationship. We weren't best pals or anything, but we didn't want to rip out each other's guts either. He didn't care about my past. He didn't pity me like a lot of people did; he didn't care what I had gone through. I wasn't glass to him. He wasn't afraid to trade insults with me, and that's what I appreciated."

"And Antonio?" Marie asked. "When did you guys meet?"

"Middle school."

"And Julian?"

Jason smiled. "I've known Julian since we were nine; we met in an orphanage. We were roommates. Jesse—my younger brother—and I were adopted when I was eleven, and a year later Julian was adopted by the same family, Erika and Ken Mattson." Jason quickly reclaimed the flames that had slowly died down before shaking the ashes from his stick. "It's cooking," he said suddenly, refusing to meet Marie's gaze. A blush enveloped his rosy cheeks. "My hobby," he informed her, "it's cooking."

❋

It had been over three hours since Mr. Marcette had walked into the forest. He had yet to return. On the beach, the rest of the Marcettes sat, some staring at the forest with a hated gaze, others glaring at the waves that crashed rhythmically on the shore.

"He just went in for food," Mrs. Marcette said quietly. "It wasn't supposed to take this long."

"He's not coming back, is he?" Marie asked with a sniff. She wrapped her shaky arms around her knees and let her head rest against her mother's shoulder.

"Then let's look for him!" William declared. "We can find him."

"And get eaten ourselves?" Diego asked.

William scowled. "It's a stupid plant!"

"A stupid plant that *kills*," Jason reminded him.

William huffed angrily and stalked off toward the rocks by the shore.

Jason followed and waited, and eventually William stopped staring at the waves and turned his saddened gaze to Jason.

"I won the tickets, Jason. I brought them here. My family's here because of me. Mark is *dead* because of *me*! My father ... If I had never listened to that contest ..." William wiped at his face.

"You're not the only one who feels like this," Jason said. He lifted a hand to squeeze William's shoulder but let it waver in the air instead. "Julian ..."

"Julian is our never-ending optimist!" William interrupted. "You can't tell me he feels the same way!"

Jason traced the dirt beside him, aware of the skeptical stare he was receiving as he dotted the eyes on his happy face. He sighed drearily before covering the childish image with his palm and smoothing the picture into nothingness. "When we were younger, Julian told me he wanted to be a clown. He said the world was such a terrible place already; it could do without more frowns and tears. He wanted to make people smile when they were having a bad day. He wanted to make them forget their troubles and bask in the innocence of naïve laughter. If he could help someone out—and it didn't matter who it was—he would be happy. Julian likes to see people with a smile on their face, and if they can't manage one, he'll put one on for them." Jason was silent for a moment, staring at Julian from where they sat. "Julian's far from happy. He blames himself for Sandy and Antonio's deaths."

"But they weren't his fault!"

Jason nodded in agreement. "Is it your fault about Mark and your father?"

William faltered. Finally, he shook his head. "No."

"Will you stop blaming yourself?" Jason's concerned eyes trailed after William as he stood, dusting his tattered clothes of sandy dirt. "William? Will you?"

William never answered.

12

Julian silently stared at Anitaa as she lay on the sand, thrashing in her sleep. He could sympathize with the nightmares; they haunted him too. He left his perch and gently grasped her smaller shoulders, shaking her awake. He shifted when her eyes snapped open and breathed deeply.

"You were moaning in your sleep," he said in offer of an explanation.

"Antonio—I had a dream about Antonio."

Julian didn't ask for more, and Anitaa didn't expand. Their attention was drawn by the sound of splashing. "I think I'll join Will and Mrs. Marcette," she said quietly. "I could go for a swim."

Julian watched Anitaa wade into the water and smiled. The moment she left, Marie filled her spot.

"I have nightmares too," she said and glared at the ocean. "I dream about Mark and Dad and—well, you sometimes."

Julian was startled and turned his gaze to Marie. "Excuse me?"

"You always die a few feet away from me. Every time I try to save you, you move farther and farther until you disappear altogether. You die over and over again, and now I can't help but wonder if this is a dream, and in a moment something will come out of the forest and take you away, and I'll never see you again."

Julian stretched his arm over her shoulder and pulled her closer. Marie sniffed but made no effort to shrug away.

"Marie," he said softly, concern mingling with distress, "this is no dream. This is real."

"What are your nightmares about?" Marie asked, and Julian could tell she was trying to get away from talking about herself.

"My family," he said in a quiet voice. This time it was him who chose to look away.

"Why would you have nightmares about your family? Everyone loves their families."

Julian chuckled, but it was no sound of amusement. It was void and mirthless, and hearing the sound emerge from his lips was eerie. "Not me. If you knew … My father was a murderer. He killed … he killed two people very important to me."

"Is he still …?"

"Suicide," Julian said in a clipped voice.

"Get out of the water!" Jason cried suddenly, interrupting the uncomfortable conversation. He was sprinting toward them. Three thick stubs of green shot out of the forest and pierced through the water.

Julian glanced at the ocean and then cringed back in surprise.

Anitaa was gone.

"Out of the water!" Jason yelled again, sounding more desperate. "Get out of the water!"

"Mom!" Marie screamed as Mrs. Marcette was pulled underneath the jolting waves. Her fingertips surfaced for barely a second, hovering over the water before disappearing into the blackened depths.

Marie let out a choked whimper.

"William! William, move!" Jason cried from the shore.

William began to splash hurriedly toward the shore. His eyes widened and his arms flapped around him before he took a deep breath and disappeared.

Jason dropped to his knees and grabbed the nearest rock. He began to slam it against the plant, hacking away at the closest green tentacle. "It's trying to drown them!"

The rock was now slippery as his blood mixed with the yellowish-green juice of the plant. The vine jerked. Diego began to claw away at the second vine with his nails. The vine nearest Jason retracted slowly, dragging a weakly struggling William from the ocean floor.

William gasped in air and continued to thrash, his efforts diminishing as he was pulled across the clinging sand. Jason leaped from his spot and grabbed William's hands, hooking his feet around a large rock.

With a squelching sound, the vine ripped, and the two fell to the sand, panting in exhaustion. The vine slithered back into the forest, leaving a gooey trail of liquid in its wake.

The part of the plant fastened to William's legs twitched violently. William rolled to his side and began to cough.

Jason crawled to William's feet and ripped the vine away. He glanced to the side just in time to see the remaining vines emerge from the sea.

"Anitaa!" Julian cried and broke away from Marie, making a miraculous jump for Anitaa's hand but missing by inches. He landed on his stomach, staring as the hand bumped along in the sand. It looked as though Anitaa was waving for the last time. He sat up. His legs were sprawled in front of him as he watched the forest in horror, groaning into his hands angrily. The ground trembled underneath them, and a feeling not unlike an earthquake suddenly took over. The sand in front of Julian began to shake, tumbling across miniature dunes.

"Julian! Move!" Jason cried.

A vine broke free from the ground and towered over Julian, its end cocked in fury as it rose with an unnatural stillness. Julian began to back away slowly.

"Stop moving!" exclaimed Mr. Razat.

Julian froze, watching the vine intently.

"It can't hear or see you. It's feeling the vibrations on the ground!" Mr. Razat turned to address the others. "No one move!"

Julian gulped as the vine lowered itself to the sand. It crawled toward him like a snake to its prey, circling and trapping him, cutting off all routes of escape.

"J-Jason?" Julian stuttered, trembling as the vine began to curl around his legs, locking them together. He squeezed his eyes shut. His breath hitched in his throat as the vine began to coil around him slowly, the sharp thorns dragging red lines across his bruised skin. Julian tried not to wince but couldn't help a slight tremble.

The vine began to retreat, dragging an ensnared Julian after it.

"Help!" cried Julian. He struggled fiercely with the prickling vine, cringing in pain as the thorns pierced his skin.

"Cut him free!" Jason ordered as he slammed a rock into the vine. He grasped the dripping cut and pulled, tearing the vine in two. He gently tore the vine from Julian's feet.

"Is he okay?" Marie asked.

Jason ran a hand over his forehead, wiping the sweat that had gathered.

"He'll be fine. He's not bleeding that bad—just his hands." Jason quickly ripped a piece of his shirt and tore the fabric into two strips, wrapping the cloth around Julian's bloody palms.

"I can speak for myself," Julian muttered, but he sounded a bit out of it.

Mr. Razat lit a fire without a word and encircled the flames with stones.

"Why?" Marie asked quietly. Her eyes were glazed with a silvery sheen, and she seemed to be unaware that she had spoken aloud. "We were easier targets; why didn't it take us?"

"Go to sleep, Marie," Jason said, instead of answering. "And you, Julian, Diego, go to sleep. Mr. Razat, you're keeping watch with me."

Julian refused to follow Jason's brash orders. "Jason …"

"No," Jason said before Julian could protest. "You're sleeping. I don't care what you say, and I don't care if you don't like it. You are going to lie next to that fire and close your eyes."

"Good … good night, Jason," muttered Marie, as she settled next to her brother, paying no attention to the look of surprise that flitted across Jason's face. She paused for a second before sitting up with a determined expression. "Wake me up in a few hours, and I'll take over."

13

Light drops trickled from the sky, sending ripples through the glistening ocean. Marie was leaning against her brother's shoulder, neither seemingly bothered by the light shower of rain. Together, they stared at the angry gray clouds that adorned the sky, both drifting in and out of their own complex thoughts. In front of them, Jason paced relentlessly. He'd stop every now and then to cast a nervous glance toward the forest. Julian was perched on a low rock, cross-legged and eyeing Jason with casual interest as the teenager continued his hurried strides. Diego and his father had taken shelter by a tree that separated sand from forest.

"Do you think anyone will ever find us?" asked Marie. She flung the wet strands of hair from her eyes and shivered from the cold.

"Sometimes we should hope for the best," said Julian, "but prepare for the worst."

"We're running low on food," said Jason as he pointed to the bundle beside Julian—two sweet fruits they still hadn't named and a couple of reddish berries they had stumbled upon. A bottle half-filled with boiled water was stuck into the sand, and beside it was a container filled with the few matches they had left.

"We can't do anything about it," said Mr. Razat, as he and Diego approached the others and he nodded toward the forest. "One step in there, and you're dead. It's been picking us off one by one, and sooner or later, we're going to be attacked—*again*."

"I'm not going in there," William agreed. "I'm not going, and you can't make me."

"None of us *wants* to go in there, William, but would you rather starve?" said Jason pointedly.

"Will, he's right. We need food," agreed Marie.

"We're going to have to take chances—*risks*—if we want to stay alive," added Julian. "Yes, that *thing* lives in the forest, but it isn't immobile! We all saw it take … the others … from the ocean. I'm sure it could do that to us at any moment."

Jason walked briskly toward one of the towering trees and snapped one of the lower branches off of its limb. He searched the ground and scooped a handful of rocks, thumbing through them.

"Jason?" asked Mr. Razat. "What are you doing?"

Jason flashed a pointed stone in his fingers before bringing it to the tip of the branch and peeling away a rough layer of olden bark. "These will work better than the rocks alone, don't you think?" Jason examined the slightly sharper tip. "Aren't any of you going to help?"

Diego was the first to rush forward, breaking another branch with a bit more difficulty and then taking longer to find a decently shaped rock. He studied Jason's graceful actions before shakily imitating his method of skinning the thin branch.

Julian stifled a sigh from the side and raised his hands, showing the ragged bandages adorning his palms.

"And what am I supposed to do? Sit and recite Shakespeare?" He winced as he stretched the tender skin, noticing the slight reddening beneath the rough fabric.

"I don't see why not," said Jason.

"So wise, so young," said Julian, pointing his annoyed stare in Jason's direction, "they say do never live long."

"Okay, I probably deserved that," Jason admitted, as he fingered the sharp edge of the branch and smiled. He threw the stick to the ground and broke another one. "But Julian, what do you think you can do with your hands? I can see the red stains, so stop trying to hide them."

"Marie," William muttered. "Go sit with Julian. We don't want him brooding."

Marie stood and brushed the dirt off her clothes. She sat on the sand beside Julian, using a finger to play with the muddied sand.

"I'm not a kid. I don't need any of you to look after me."

"I'm not here to look after you," said Marie as she cupped her hands and buried them in the water near her feet. "How long do you think we've been here?"

"Three weeks, five days, and eight hours."

Marie jumped back in alarm. "You've been keeping track?"

Julian shook his head and raised his right arm, showing her the small watch that dangled from his wrist. The face was broken, and the hands had stopped ticking a long time ago, now resting on the ten and one.

"The water got to mine, and I doubt any of us have a working watch. After a while the days don't seem to matter anymore. At first I tried to keep track, but nothing made sense. I don't even know if today's Monday or Thursday, much less if it's been two weeks or three. I just tackle each day separately. It no longer matters, what day it is. What matters is whether or not I'll live to see the next dawn."

Marie nodded to the watch, examining the fine tracings that covered the silver band and face. "If it's broken then why don't you take it off?"

Julian shook his head, fingering the fragile object with a trace of distress. "It was my mother's."

Both teenagers jumped when two sharpened sticks clattered in front of them. They looked up in fright to see Jason standing over them.

"Come on, you two lovebirds, we're leaving."

✺

Marie scrutinized the sky above her, watching as the clouds were gently blown across it. The moon was shinning once more—halfway full. Still, as long as they were not alone in the dark, Marie would try to remain content. The slivery light drifted down, moonbeams lighting dark shafts all around them. Marie gasped suddenly and felt around for anyone she could reach. Grabbing what she suspected to be a shoulder, she began to shake the nearest person frantically.

"Eh?" Diego groaned and rolled over, but the ruthless waking continued. He opened one eye and squinted. "Marie, go to sleep," he moaned quietly before closing his eyes.

"Diego," said Marie. She pulled him up and slapped his arm a few times. "Am I losing it, or is that star blinking?"

Diego's sleepily eyes shot open and widened considerably. "Marie," he said slowly, "that's not a star, that's a *plane*!" He scrambled to his feet and ran toward Jason, waving his hands in the air with renewed energy. "A plane! A plane is up there!"

Jason's head tipped upward before a grin erupted. He ran toward the silver container and grabbed a couple of matches, dropping them into the fire. The flames sparked and soared higher.

"Help!" Marie screamed. "Help! We're down here!" Her cries quickly mixed in with the other shrieks around her.

"Hey!" Mr. Razat roared, grabbing a branch and sticking it into the fire. Once the tip was ignited, he pulled it out and began to swirl it in the air. "Turn around, we're down here!"

"Don't get your hopes up; it's gone," whispered William, sinking into the muddy sand.

Marie shook her head in determination, clutching both hands to her chest as she searched the night sky for every detail. Her eyes lingered on every star she could find. "They…they probably went to get help! They must've seen the fire." Her eyes sought Julian's, and she was surprised to see him sitting next to Jason, both looking crestfallen. She took William's hand and approached the fire. They sat across from the duo, all in ominous silence, until William's desolate sigh tore their attention.

"We need to take our minds off it," said William softly. He looked up, a half-smile forming on his pale lips. "Tell us how you two met."

"In an orphanage," Julian said.

"What happened to your parents?"

"William!" Marie hissed into his ear. "Honestly!"

"It's all right," Jason said, and Julian nodded. "My parents died when I was nine; Jesse was two. A drunk driver hit them. Both sides of my family had been against the marriage, so Jesse and I weren't wanted. We went to an orphanage, and that's where we met Julian."

"We *hated* each other," Julian said. He was smiling. "We were roommates, and after being in about thirteen different foster homes and orphanages, I was sick of it all. I refused to talk to Jason, so he hacked into my computer file and made a comment about my family."

"He punched me," exclaimed Jason. "After a few months of fighting we … reconciled. I was adopted when I was eleven, and a year later I convinced my adoptive parents—Erica and Ken—to adopt Julian and then, voilà: a happy—if a bit messed up—family."

"Julian," William said soberly, "you never answered my question. What happened to *your* parents?"

Marie straightened, eyes wide at her brother's blunt question. "William!"

Julian smiled sadly. He stood and stretched. "I'll have to answer that question later I'm afraid. I'm simply too tired at the moment." He faked a yawn before stumbling away from the roaring flames.

Marie watched as his shallow breathing became deeper, but it was uncertain whether he was feigning sleep. "Who did his father kill?"

William glanced up, startled.

Jason sighed heavily and bent, grabbing a stick and stroking the wood in the fire. "He told you."

It was far from a question—more a statement than anything. Marie nodded and was stunned to see Jason rub his eyes. By now his mask of emotions was gone, and instead of the controlling authority he was known for, Jason appeared like a little child who had gotten lost in a grocery store. The shadows under his eyes contrasted against his pasty skin, which was marred with lines of fatigue and stress.

"What did he tell you?"

"Only that his father killed two people he was really close too and then committed suicide. But he said he was in thirteen different foster homes and orphanages, right? And that means that something must have happened to his mother. Maybe she left them, but the way Julian speaks about his family ..."

"He talked about his sister though," said William. "I don't think he realized I was there. He said something like, 'She would be fifteen right now.' He mentioned her name—Madelyn? Marcie? I know it started with a ..."

"Madison," Jason said quietly.

"You know, then?"

"Do I know?" Jason repeated. "Is that a serious question? I'm his brother; what do you think?"

"Adoptive brother," said William softly.

Marie was surprised by the look of anger that fleeted across Jason's face.

"Does that matter? As far as I am concerned, Julian is my brother, and I'm his."

"What happened to Madison?" asked Marie. "He said she would be fifteen? *Would*? Does that mean she's dead too?"

"Would you stop talking about it?" asked Jason.

"She must be dead!" William exclaimed. "And if he said his father killed two people, he was close to—"

"—and his mother could be dead—"

"—which would mean his father—"

"—killed them both!"

"Shut up!" Jason hissed. "Stop trying to pry your way into things neither of you could ever understand!"

"I'm the same age as you!" said William defiantly.

"That might be true, but we have *very* different lives, William. Before this *vacation*," Jason spat the word out, "you probably knew nothing of death.

Julian and I have been dealing with it for longer than any of you could ever imagine. Secrets are *secrets* for a reason!"

"But is it true?" William persisted.

"What if it is?" Jason growled. "Julian doesn't need your pity; he's had enough of it. Yes, his father killed his mother and sister—and *yes*, the coward killed himself. You don't need to know the details." Jason stood briskly.

"Wait," Marie whispered before he could get too far. "How old was Julian when he …How old was he when they all died?"

Jason squared his shoulders. "Eight."

Marie tensed next to William as Jason left. "Will? It's just me and you now, isn't it? What do you think will happen when we get back? Will we go to an orphanage like …?"

William looked up with a soft stare and took her smaller hands into his own. "Of course not, Marie; Aunt Silvia and Uncle Perry will take us in. They're our godparents." He wrapped his arms around her shoulders and laid his chin on her head. "Don't worry," he said, pinching her cheek lightly and smiling when she batted his hand from her face. "I'm not going to let anything happen to you."

"Promise?"

William hooked a pinky around hers with an ease of experience. "Promise, and since when have I broke my promises?"

Marie smiled because this was true. Not once had William ever broken a promise to anyone. He only gave his word when he knew he could not break it, and Marie took immense relief in that. Together, the Marcette siblings dazedly watched the roaring flames in content, pinkies loyally fastened by their sides.

14

Diego yawned deeply. His hands stretched above him, reaching for the fluffy white balls of cotton that drifted endlessly in the sky. They were sprayed with pastel pink, and a soft, golden yellow shone through the cracks the small clouds embodied. Diego's head bent at an awkward angle, and his eyes began to droop before he snapped to attention, shaking himself awake. *He needed to stay alert.* He rubbed his eyes and began to scrutinize the dawn that had emerged from its prison minutes ago. Its thick beams trickled across the waters and glorified the sparkling sand with its welcoming shine.

Across from Diego, piled chaotically, were their futile attempts at weapons. The tips of the sharpened sticks were slightly burnt from being too close to the roaring flames.

He could hear snoring from either side of him. People were scattered around the beach instead of the tight circle they had slowly become attached to.

Jason and Julian's eyes were closed, their pale faces content, and their soft breaths were deep; but Diego would bet the clothes on his back that neither had slept during the night. The light crease across Julian's forehead and the slight tension in Jason's shoulders supplied substantial evidence. The two were so alike in personality and appearance; yet the small details that made them distinct were so prominent that none could deny.

It was like they were a different side of one coin; on one side was the rugged spiral of sharpened edges, threatening disaster to those who opposed, and on the other was the delicate side with lines so clear and calculating, so in-depth that as your eyes trailed over the swirls and textures you'd begin to lose thought, easily manipulated by the glossy silver. Jason and Julian were two people Diego would never like to cross, purposely or not. Considering the tragedy of losing one's parents, Jason's grave and unwelcoming demeanor could be excused, but what of it compared to Julian's past?

Diego and his father had heard the hushed conversation that had occurred late into the night. Both had seen Julian walk toward them, ignorant of their consciousness. They had watched as Julian's smile faded and his fists clenched beneath his head as his past was unintentionally revealed.

Now Diego's father lay next to him, his snores another reason why Diego refused to fall into a dreamless sleep.

Sleep was now a blur of dreamless gray that welcomed him into the world of slumber. Before, it had been frightening images painted with bubbling blood and laced with venomous violence. Then it had changed, its usual dark and dreary colors brightening to warm shades and dazzling tints, but that had soon faded. It was too late for dreams, and Diego was half-afraid he had lost the imagination on innocence.

His father snored again, and Diego was tempted to elbow him out of his slumber. His mouth stretched open once more, and he began to blink repeatedly, trying to find any means possible to stay awake.

Everything slowly faded from in front of him. It was as if a sudden cloud of flies had been dropped over his head, and an eerie buzzing quietly rung in his ears. Diego inclined his head at an uncomfortable angle and gazed at the sticks that had appeared in midair, dangling from invisible strings like puppets being played. They danced around him, twirling and spinning in a coordinated fashion before one reached out with its sharp end and poked him—*hard*.

"Ow!" Diego said and rubbed his arm with a look of annoyance. "Was that necessary?"

Another strong prod was issued, much to Diego's irritation. "Hey! Stop!" Diego said to the vanishing sticks and blinked as a hand became visible, holding the remaining stick tightly.

"Rub your eyes," a voice commanded, and Diego wasn't sure whether to obey the demanding tone or to search the sky for the origin of the familiar voice.

"God?" he asked tentatively and winced when a harder poke reached his shoulder.

"Not exactly."

Diego yawned and quickly rubbed his eyes, blinking past the blurs of colors as the fogginess began to fade away. And there, poised casually in front of him, smirked Jason.

"Good to see you're paying attention."

"Oh," replied Diego, and then he bolted up in alarm. "Oh god! I feel asleep, didn't I? I tried …"

"It's all right," Jason reassured him. "I was awake."

The bushes to their right rustled unexpectedly, breaking the amused silence. The boys exchanged looks before Diego stood, taking the sharpened stick Jason handed him. He cast a worried look at his father's peaceful expression, wondering what the man could be dreaming of. He turned around, and something slammed into his stomach. His arms wrapped around his midriff as he went down, groaning in pain, and his stick clattered to the sand, buried halfway between the small grains. He squinted through the shafts of light, searching for Jason. He spotted a scratched hand hidden among a clutter of rocks and struggled to rise, clutching his stomach and swallowing the vile lump that had risen in his throat.

"Jason?" he croaked. His back was hunched as he stumbled toward the motionless hand. He dropped to his knees, cringing when the sharpened rocks dug into skin. "Jason!" Glancing tentatively toward the eerily silent forest, Diego rose to his feet and scrambled toward his father, shaking the man out of his tranquil dreams.

"Diego?" Mr. Razat groaned and sat up, rubbing his eyes. "What's wrong?"

Diego thrust his branch into his father's hands and gestured toward the rocks where Jason lay. "I can't lift him. I'll wake the others while you bring him here." He hurried to the huddled group. "Marie, Will," he said, as he squatted on the balls of his feet, "come on, wake up!" Diego turned swiftly and went to grab Julian' shoulder. A hand darted out and caught Diego's fingers at the last second, and then Julian quickly pulled himself to a sitting position.

"Sorry," Julian apologized, "bad habit."

"Jason!" Marie exclaimed.

"What happened?" Julian asked. He pushed Diego out of the way and hurriedly approached Jason's side. He lowered the back of his hand against Jason's forehead and then pressed two fingers to his neck.

"I don't know," admitted Diego. "He told me that we should check around, make sure everything was okay, you know? And then I turned around and something slugged me in the stomach. By the time I could stand, Jason's hand was sticking out of those rocks."

"You didn't see who did it?"

"It had to be that *thing*."

William hushed them, staring intently at the trees that rustled in response. The smaller trees began to bow as the wind pushed through, blasting them all with frozen air.

"Look out!" yelled Mr. Razat before they were surrounded by vines, most thin and miniature in size. They swirled around the teenagers and separated them. As quick as it had started, it was over. The vines retreated into the forest leaving several of them panting in fear.

"Is everyone all right?" Jason called out. His voice sounded small and weak and fragile.

"Dad?" Diego called out.

His father limped over and wrapped his arms around him. Diego closed his eyes, content to be alive.

"Jule? Julian?" Jason scrutinized the ground below. A few grains of sand were dotted with red, trailing toward the forest. "Julian!"

"*It* took him." Marie sagged against William. Her shoulders shook as she struggled to contain her cries.

"And our food," Diego whispered in awe, eyeing the disturbed patch of sand where they stored the fruits and water. "All of it."

Only his father seemed to hear the comment. Mr. Razat turned to William. "You'll watch them … if anything happens?"

William seemed startled at the request but nodded over Marie's shoulder. His sad smile said the words he couldn't find.

Diego grabbed the few sticks that were not splintered or broken. "I'm coming with you."

His father slowly nodded and took the branch Diego offered. "We'll try to be back as soon as possible, but if we don't make it …" Mr. Razat trailed off.

"I'm glad we got to know each other," William said quietly.

Diego nodded to Marie. "When she calms down, tell Marie I'll miss her if I don't …" He choked and stepped back, shaking his head. He grasped his father's fingers as they walked through the leaves, leaving the wind to trail after them in a disdainful manner.

✺

Marie gazed blankly ahead. A whimper escaped her lips, but when William shifted closer, she inched away. Jason's eyes were wide, and his mouth formed a tiny *o*. His cheeks were stained with dirt and blood and grime and filth, but there were several clear trails that ran from his lower eyelashes to his chin where his tears had fallen.

The sun had been descending ever since Mr. Razat and Diego departed in search for food, but neither Jason nor Marie had noticed the two missing. They were wrapped in their solitary worlds, standing alone and seeing no one but themselves.

Something in the woods rustled nearby. William cast a weary eye toward Jason before chewing on his mutilated lip.

"Hey!" someone shouted in the foggy distance, and a blur of figures emerged from the crinkling bushes. William's eyes widened, and his mouth dropped open, hanging limply as he stared. "Look who we found!"

William paid the voice no attention, clearly focused on the teenager who stood, bruised, bloody, and badly injured—but *stood*—in front of him with a half-grin sitting evenly on his pale lips.

Julian wobbled forward, past a grinning William, past a shell-shocked Marie, and dropped next to Jason, unable to keep the beaming smirk off his face.

William grasped Marie's hand and pulled her to her feet, dragging her away from the duo. Her forehead was wrinkled in unspoken confusion, and William shook his head, wrapping his arms around her trembling body. "After."

"I hope you're not thinking about coffee again," Julian murmured.

Jason's mouth hung further, and his fingers tightened around the sand he was clutching. White spots danced around his knuckles. "J-Julian?" he said in a small voice. A genuine smile broadened against his lips, and he threw his arms around Julian, squeezing his eyes shut. "You're alive!" he exclaimed in a whisper, his voice cracking slightly.

"I told you before that you can't get rid of me that easily," said Julian. He smiled and tightened the hug, forcing his body not to shake from exhaustion and pain. Julian ignored the stings that burnt through his skin, ignored the blood that dripped down his hand, and ignored the throbbing ache that had begun to pound against his head. All that mattered was that he was alive. He had beaten the plant; he had *won*.

❖

Marie glared at her blurred reflection, examining the cuts that littered her face with distaste. Tentatively, she reached out and ran a finger along her cheek, frowning when she traced the bloodied skin. She turned away, desperate to avoid the emerald eyes that stared back at her through the pearly water.

"Penny for your thoughts?"

Marie jumped and noticed Julian's figure in the watery reflection. "Only a penny?" she asked, mirroring Julian's soft tone. She watched as Julian's reflection sat close to hers and suddenly felt a tingling sensation in her stomach.

They sat in silence, neither wanting to upset the soothing beauty that had settled around them.

"I thought you were dead," Marie finally whispered. "We all did." No tears gathered at the corner of her eyes; she was done with crying.

"I know," was all Julian said.

"When you disappeared, I regretted that I never told you how I felt and that whatever I had hoped for was gone. And I made myself promise that, if you came back, I would tell you, and here you are." Marie smiled weakly. "I think I'm falling in love with you." She averted her eyes and wrapped her arms around herself. She turned away from Julian and glowered at her reflection.

The silence was deafening as Julian stared at Marie. A look of clear surprise was plastered to his face.

Her forehead wrinkled and she frowned, dropping Julian's hand. "I must look terrible," she commented. She would give anything to make the silence go away.

"I think you look beautiful," said Julian as he nudged closer, smiling sincerely. They stared at each other for a long time, mesmerized.

"Aren't you going to kiss me?" Marie asked.

"Aren't we taking this a bit too fast?"

"Julian, we could die at any moment. What else can we do, if not fast?"

"We can enjoy time together," Julian suggested, and Marie smiled.

"I'd like that."

❋

"Dad."

Mr. Razat smiled.

Diego shifted and began to fidget with what was left of his sleeves. "I've been meaning to tell you something …. Any day here could be our last because, at any moment, we might lose each other."

"Right," said Mr. Razat. He nodded as he stared off into the distance. There was a slight crinkle lining his forehead.

"Well," Diego continued, "I know that the two of us have never been as close as we should, and we haven't said this as much as we'd like. But just so you know, Dad, I love you." He shifted awkwardly.

"Eh? Diego?" Mr. Razat glanced up. "Did you say something?"

Diego sighed and shook his head. "No," he murmured, loud enough for Mr. Razat to hear, "nothing important."

He walked past his father and cringed when Marie spotted him. He tried to quicken his speed, but she caught up.

"Diego!"

"Marie," Diego whispered quietly, "can't you just leave me alone?"

Marie glanced at Diego in confusion. She took his hand and pulled him toward the tides. The white foam hurdled through the sea and crashed to the sandy shore. The fresh and salty smell danced forward, burning their nostrils with a crisp scent.

"I hate him," Diego whispered suddenly, his lidded eyes pointing in his father's direction. "I really hate him. And he hates me—don't say otherwise, Marie; you don't even know us." If Diego had looked up at that moment, he would have seen the wounded expression Marie didn't bother to hide. Instead, Diego frowned and wrinkled his chin.

"Diego, I'm sure that's not true," was all Marie could say.

"Sal was closer to him; she was his favorite. He loved her like *mama* loved me, and now they're both gone," Diego shuddered and cast an angry and fleeting look toward his father, "and we're stuck with each other."

Marie's mouth opened and closed. She stood up lividly, and he followed, matching her stare of disbelief with irritation. "You—you—you—" she stuttered, too outraged to piece together words. "You idiot!"

"Marie?"

"I've lost both of my parents here, Diego! *Both* of them! My mom and dad, gone! And Mark, gone! Your dad is still alive, and you're feeling sorry for yourself?"

"Marie," Diego pleaded, "I didn't mean ..."

"I'm not finished!" She no longer made an effort to lower her voice. "You," she spat spitefully before raising her voice, "I thought you were better than that! You think he *hates* you?" Her laugh was bleak and empty. "From what I've seen between you two during our *oh-so-pleasant stay*, is that that man," she pointed to Mr. Razat, "loves you just as much as he loves Salatina, and you should feel damn lucky to have a parent who is still alive and can take care of you!"

"Take care of me?" Diego scoffed, crossing his arms over his chest. "How the hell can *he* take care of *me*?"

Marie ignored him and stalked off, heading toward the other teenagers and trying not to tremble.

"You okay?" William asked,

"Stupid idiot," Marie muttered into her hand and turned around. She watched Diego's stiffened form.

"What is he doing?" Julian asked.

"Not *what* is he doing," Jason quietly said. "What does he *think* he's doing?"

The four froze, watching as Diego smiled sadly at them and broke into a run, heading straight for the forest.

15

As soon as Diego entered the forest, Mr. Razat sprung to his feet and followed. He ignored the other teenagers, frantically trailing his son.

"Jason!" Marie cried as she stared after the Razats. "Aren't you going to go after them?"

Jason wanted to say yes—in his mind, he was screaming the word over and over again—but he couldn't. He couldn't endanger any more lives, and he knew that was exactly what would happen if they followed. Silently, because at that moment his voice had deserted him, Jason shook his head and crossed his arms, knowing he'd appear emotionless.

"Jason, they could be killed! Are you even listening to us?"

"Why don't you listen to yourself?" he bellowed. He rigidly gestured toward the greenery that waved scornfully before them. "They're as good as dead! They're no longer our problem!" He faced the ocean, unable to look at the betrayed stares he knew were behind him. No doubt Julian would be frowning disappointedly.

"If you want to give up, go ahead. But I remember someone telling me they would *never* leave friends behind."

Marie's words hit harder than expected, leaving Jason to stubbornly blink back the tears that were brimming in his eyes.

"You didn't have to be such a jerk." Julian's voice cut through the air better than a razor-sharp knife ever could.

"I wasn't being a jerk," Jason responded, reluctant to turn around. When he did, he was met with the same disappointing frown he had predicted. He hated that.

"You could have been nicer about it," said Julian.

"Why do you care?"

"They're my friends."

"You hardly know them!"

"I may not know them as well as I know you," Julian said with a soft but biting voice, "but I know enough to realize who my friends are, and who my enemies are becoming."

Jason felt his fingers twitch as he ached to hit something. "It's either them or me," he said and squared his shoulders.

Julian raised his head. There was a torn expression sprawled across his face. "A real brother would never ask me to choose." Julian turned around, walking slowly toward the trees.

Jason stood for a moment, frozen as Julian's words assaulted mercilessly. "You know you'll probably die."

Julian just raised a hand in acknowledgment and let it fall to his side.

Jason sighed and followed Julian into the forest. "And you're taking me with you."

※

Mr. Razat raced through the bushes. He ignored the stinging sensation as branches scratched against his skin. He paused to catch his breath, leaning on his knees as his chest heaved. He raised a hand to his forehead and wiped the sticky sweat away. He glanced at the sky and blinked when a wet drop hit his cheek.

"That's not right," he whispered. He brought a finger to wipe away the droplet. He glanced at his hand and froze, eyes tracing the smudged crimson that stained his fingers. He gulped fearfully and tilted his head to the heavens.

Above him swayed a branch. Its end was painted in red, and it brandished a ripped cloth that flapped contentedly in the wind. The checkered pattern rang a familiar bell in his memory, and Mr. Razat dashed through the forest once more, trying not to think of why a piece of his son's sweater was lodged high in a tree.

"Help!" he heard Diego cry.

Mr. Razat looked around for any more blood, searching the trees, the leaves, and the ground. Nothing was broken or out of place. The forest had gone deathly still, and Mr. Razat paused, wondering if the scream for help had only been his imagination.

"Dad!"

Mr. Razat's head snapped up, and his eyes widened as a smile broke out. He *knew* he hadn't imagined *that*.

"Diego, where are ..."

Something didn't let Mr. Razat finish. The next thing he saw was the dirt trail as his face hit it, smacking loudly against the ground. He struggled to stay conscious, blinking repeatedly to wave away the black spots that danced around his line of vision. He was briefly aware he was being dragged backward, but his mind would not register his dilemma. Something prickly pierced the skin on his legs.

"Dad!" he heard again, and this time Mr. Razat tried to answer. His mouth opened and closed, but it was as though someone had hit the mute button. No sound would come out. He formed a name on his lips but the energy to move his jaw was too much, and he let his head sag wearily. His vision blurred slightly, and the trees above him took on new shapes, swirling around in a colorful pattern before mixing with the crystal blue sky.

"Dad!"

Mr. Razat must have imagined the voice because now it seemed closer than before.

"Don't worry," the imaginary voice said.

Mr. Razat wondered why it seemed so familiar.

"Don't give up! I'm going to help you, Dad!"

The pricking feeling was quickly replaced by a burning so intense that Mr. Razat was confident his legs were on fire. He was pulled forward this time; he could feel hands clutching his torn shirt, hauling him gently.

"Don't worry, Dad; you're going to be fine."

"Ugh," Mr. Razat moaned and reached out, grasping a soft cloth and yanking with surprising strength. He opened his eyes and stared at the glowing figure inches away from his face, gleaming with pure intent.

It was an angel.

"Hel—" Mr. Razat paused, doubting the words he was about to form. "Hello?"

The angel's face glowed with joy, and it rushed forward, wrapping its arms around him and squeezing tightly.

"Dad," the angel whispered, "I thought you were dead!"

Mr. Razat wanted to reach over and wipe away the angel's pearly tears, but his arms felt like weights.

"Don't cry," Mr. Razat said, trying to make the angel feel better. He sent it a lopsided grin, hoping to receive one in return. Instead of mirroring his action, the angel frowned in misery.

"Dad?"

Mr. Razat was clearly confused but smiled despite it. He struggled to lift his right hand, dragging it until it rested on top of the angel's. He squeezed it softly, beaming as he studied the angel.

"Stop," he whispered gently. "You don't have to weep for me."

The angel sniffed loudly.

Mr. Razat sighed and leaned his head against the rough bark. "Aren't you going to take me soon?"

"Take you where?" the angel asked in obvious distress, wiping its tears away.

"To heaven, of course," he wheezed slightly. "You're here to take me, right? I want to go ... I want to see my family again—"

"Dad," the angel interrupted. "Dad, you're delirious—"

"No," Mr. Razat exclaimed. "Let me finish." He was silent for a moment as he struggled to collect his thoughts. "The ... the darkness is settling in—this place ... it's a bad place. I ... I want to leave. I want to be with my family. And that's good ... because you're here to take me there ... aren't you?"

"Dad—"

"But my son ... Diego ... I wish ... I could see ... Diego ... again." His breaths became shallower, but he continued on. "You look ... a lot like him ... you know?"

The angel sobbed quietly and Mr. Razat tried to shake his head, only succeeding in rolling it to one side and back.

"I ... love him ... but I don't think ... he knows that." He turned toward the angel. "Can you ... do me a ... favor?" His words were becoming slurred, but it was important that he spoke his mind before his death.

The angel nodded.

"I ... don't think ... you need to ... take me. I-I think ... I can find ... the ... way on my ... own." He squeezed the angel's hand again, and his eyes fluttered. "Find ... my son ... Diego ... please?"

The angel choked back a sob.

"Tell ... him ... love ... always ..." Mr. Razat's voice trailed off as his last breath left his body, leaving behind an empty shell, and a lone angel that sobbed beside it.

❂

"Diego?" Marie glanced at her brother, biting her lip in hesitation.

William smiled reassuringly before cupping a hand around his mouth. "Diego! Mr. Razat?" He faced Marie, running a dirty hand through his wild hair. "Any sign?"

Marie shook her head. She jumped when she heard another creak. "Will?"

William shushed Marie with a finger before glancing behind him. Gently but firmly, he grasped Marie's arms and pulled her in front of him, clasping her shoulders and squeezing tightly. He leaned down to whisper, not pausing in their footing.

"Don't run; it tracks us by our movements, remember?"

Marie nodded stiffly as William guided her. "We're going to die, aren't we?" she whispered.

"Marie," William exclaimed suddenly. He spun Marie to the right, turning her so swiftly that she almost fell. "Look over there!" he announced and quickened their pace.

Marie glanced at where William pointed and gasped, perceiving the warm burst of light with pleasure. She heard a crack, louder than before, and fearfully glanced behind her as they ran. Branches were swinging without wind, and though there were no signs of the carnivorous plant she could hear it as it swerved through trees, easily matching their pace.

"Will!" Marie cried and stumbled as William dragged her toward the opening.

"Hold on, Marie!"

Marie looked behind her, screaming when she saw the vine race toward them. "Will!" She dug her nails into William's arm. As they neared the light, she was torn away from him and thrown to the ground, landing face-first in the sand and rolling with the fast momentum. She coughed as the sand entered her mouth and shook her head, trying to clear away the dizziness. "Will," she choked out, rising unsteadily to her hands and knees. She listened for an answer quietly, trying to regain her breath. When she was met with silence, her eyes snapped open, and frantically, she searched the area, to no avail. She turned her head toward the forest, and tears began to blur her vision. "Will!"

❀

Jason trudged behind Julian, reluctant to be searching for the others. Julian was calling out names, concerned as always. Jason hadn't called out once. It wasn't that he didn't care. He just didn't see the point.

A swish to the right grabbed Jason's attention, and a scraping sound echoed off the trunks around him. "Julian, hold on," he said as he peered through the numerous branches. He cocked his eyebrows in confusion and stepped closer to a bushy plant, reaching forward and parting it cautiously. It was just a branch scraping against the tree's bark in the wind, nothing to be worried about. He stood and turned around. Where had Julian gone? He glanced at the soft dirt and noticed the shallow footsteps that were pressed into the ground.

"Julian?" He saw Julian standing a few feet away, back facing him as he leaned against a tree. "Would it be so hard for you to answer me?" he asked, clearly annoyed.

Julian didn't respond.

Jason frowned and stepped forward, gripping Julian's shoulder and swinging him around. "Jule—what the hell happened?"

Julian's forehead was matted with hair and blood, and a fresh cut stretched from the corner of his left eye to his hairline. His arm hung limply, and it was obvious something was broken by the way Julian held it. Julian shrugged tiredly, opening his eyes. "I can't remember."

"You can't remember?" Jason asked in concern, peering into Julian's eyes to observe his pupils. "I think you have a concussion—"

"I'm tired, Jase," Julian slurred and yawned, sinking to the ground. "So … tired."

Jason shook his head. Questions reeled in his mind. "You can't sleep." Jason peered at Julian's limp arm and ran his fingers along the limb.

"Ow," Julian muttered and looked up in confusion. "What are you doing?"

Jason frowned, feeling the bones. "I'm trying to see if anything is broken."

"My wrist hurts," Julian offered and yawned again.

Nodding, Jason ripped a length of cloth from the bottom of his shirt. He looked around and grabbed a thick branch from above, breaking it into two smaller pieces. He clutched the sharp rock he had kept on his person and began to skin the wood, trying to work as quickly as possible.

"So you don't remember anything?" he asked in an attempt to keep Julian awake.

"No, I don't," Julian said, almost angrily.

Jason nodded, wincing when he sliced his finger. He refused to stop, switching the wood from one hand to the other and continuing.

"Wait," Julian said and leaned his head against Jason's shoulder. "I fell down some rocks, lots of rocks. Something tripped me."

"Don't you mean *you* tripped over something?"

"*Something* tripped *me*. I know it."

Jason lifted the somewhat smooth and thin rectangular block of wood to the sky, examining it. "Give me your wrist." Jason used the two pieces of wood as a splint, wrapping the cloth tightly around his injury. Julian was breathing heavily by the time Jason finished.

"Come on," Julian said slowly, "we need to find the others and get out."

Jason gripped Julian's arms, steadying him. "What if they're dead?"

"I ... I don't believe that, Jason. But ... if they are dead ... well ... we'll cross that bridge when we come to it."

"We're already at that bridge, Julian! We're in the middle of it!"

"I'm not leaving them," Julian said firmly. He panted slightly as he used the tree behind him as support.

"You're not leaving them, or you're not leaving *her*?"

"This has nothing to do with Marie—"

"This has *everything* to do with Marie!" Jason yelled, interrupting Julian. "I know you! You're not looking for William or Diego *or* Mr. Razat. You're looking for Marie. You *think* you love her, but I bet you don't know a thing about her."

Julian's stubborn expression crumbled to dust, and he stared at Jason painfully. "I love her," said Julian. "And don't you dare accuse me of ignoring the others! All of us have been through so much together. We've grown closer; we've become some sort of family." Julian smiled and rubbed his arm. "I've always wanted a family."

"You have a family," said Jason quietly. "Me," he pointed to himself, "and you," he pointed to Julian, "and Jesse—we're brothers. And Ken and Emily, they're our parents. *We're* your family."

"I know that. But Diego, and William, and ... What if it was Anitaa and Antonio and Sandy out there? Wouldn't you continue? Or would you run away?"

"I'm not running!"

"And neither am I."

Jason jumped when a loud bang echoed from behind. He whirled around, carefully searching for anything that seemed out of place. No leaves were scattered; no branches askew—not a thing seemed wrong. He sighed wearily and turned around, stumbling back in horror. Julian was gone, and on the tree he had been leaning against was a bloody and smeared handprint.

❋

Diego stumbled from the musky grove, desperate to be away from his father's corpse. He slid down a trunk, paying no attention to the bark that viciously dug into his back. He pressed his face into his dirty palms, and his shoulders shook as he struggled to contain his cries.

"Something happy," he whispered to himself. "Think of a happy memory, and everything will be all right." He wrapped his arms around his knees and pressed his chest closer, curling into a small ball. He closed his eyes and breathed deeply, thinking of what things would be like if he were home.

His mother would be in their living room, behind her easel with tiny brushes stuck behind both ears. The warm sun would be streaming through their bay window, lighting the area with a soft, golden glow. Soft music would be playing in the background, and his mother would be humming along in tranquility as she mixed colors and carefully skimmed a portion of the pale paper with the bristles of her brush.

His father would be in his office, if not at work. Papers would be strewn out in front of him, layered with other sheets of vast information. A gramophone would be in the corner, playing a sweet symphony of Beethoven; his father was a sucker for classics.

Salatina would be tightening taps or wiring computers. She was a genius when it came to technology. Her fingers would be a blur as she worked, never stopping until she had completed her task. She was the fix-it person everyone came to for help; their mother was clueless in that area, and their father would be so technical that what would take five minutes for Salatina would take five days for him.

And Diego—he would never be far from his twin; they always stuck close together.

He would be sitting on the couch talking about the latest prank he had pulled or the funniest thing he had thought of during the day.

As the thought of home faded, so did Diego's happiness. He didn't want to be alone anymore. He wanted to be with his family.

A prickling feeling danced through his legs, and he brushed a hand down the limb. A wave of dizziness assaulted him, and he groaned, closing his eyes as he felt a sudden wave of nausea. He sighed, noticing the trees above him beginning to move and blend in with each other, twirling around. The sky erupted in color, light beams streaming from the clouds and flickering. He tilted his head slightly, astonished to find the bark no longer against his back. *He was moving.* The plant had finally found him.

Despite the fear he felt at the thought of dying, Diego couldn't help but smile. He would be reunited with his family once more, and then he would never be alone again.

❂

"Will!" Marie cried loudly. She was desperate to hear anything other than the frightening silence that surrounded her. She kicked sand about as she sharply turned right and left, unsure of which direction to go. "William!" she yelled again. Her eyes met the forest with agitation. She was hesitant to return. "Where are you?" she muttered to herself as she hurried forward, swaying dangerously. The day was beginning to take its toll on her and she was already running low on energy. Her knees buckled and she was barely aware of someone calling her name. Strong arms encircled her waist before she reached the ground, and she was suddenly lifted like a bride.

"Are you okay?"

"Julian?" Marie asked faintly, reaching around her savior's neck

"Not exactly."

Marie tensed, suddenly feeling very awkward. Her eyes flew open, and her arms shot back toward her chest.

"Um, hello."

"Hi," Marie responded as Jason set her on her feet. She swayed dizzily before grabbing a branch above her for support. "Where's Julian? Did something happen to him? Is he all right?"

Jason's lips tightened into a thin line, and his shoulders slumped. "To be honest, I thought you were him."

"What happened?"

"We were talking, and there was this loud bang. I thought a tree fell. I turned around, and when I looked back, Julian was gone."

"You lost him?"

Jason's face twisted into something unpleasant. "I didn't lose him!" He sounded livid that she'd think of such a thing. "He was taken from me."

"William too."

Jason sighed and hesitantly placed an arm around her, bringing her closer to share his body heat. "Hey," he whispered, "don't worry. We'll find them. We'll start looking right now. I'm sure they're both all right."

"Right," Marie agreed reluctantly. "Julian's already survived, so he can do it again—but what about Will?"

"Your brother is an intelligent person. He'll look after himself." Jason gently pushed Marie forward, scanning the ground for any tracks.

"What about Diego and Mr. Razat?"

Jason turned, and their eyes met, and for a moment Marie could feel the pain, the guilt, the envy, the loneliness—could feel everything Jason was drowning in. His head barely shook before Jason broke their eye contact and continued on in silence.

16

The trees swayed rhythmically with the wind, bending back and forth as if dancing leisurely. The leaves chimed like wedding bells as they brushed together and apart—crinkling noises that echoed through the forest.

A lone vine hung from a cracked branch, swaying at its own speed. The tip twitched every so often before stilling. It began to slip off the branch, curling down the trunk as though it were a snake cautiously stalking its prey. The ground trembled with delicate vibrations, and the vine took off, slowly but steadily circling its victims.

❂

"Drag marks," Jason muttered quietly and squatted. His fingers traced the clear tracks. Blood was mixed with the dirt, and the crimson drops entwined with the grimy path. He brushed his fingers against the wet dirt and brought them closer to his face, frowning when he saw the stained skin gleam under the sunlight.

"Is it …?"

"It's one of them," he said and began to follow the tracks.

Marie trailed behind in doubt. "What if it's a trap?"

"Then we're walking right into it."

Marie hesitated for a moment before chasing after Jason. She gasped in shock, staring at the blood that smeared the bright leaves in front of her. Scarlet dripped from one leaf to another, a scarlet waterfall running through the black-tipped branches.

Jason squared his jaw and grasped Marie's hand, pulling her behind him.

Marie stared, transfixed as the drops plummeted to the ground and landed with a splatter. "You don't think they're dead … do you?"

The amount of blood was uncanny; it trickled from the trees, seeped from the leaves, oozed from the soil, and seemed to be a part of the forest itself.

"Let's keep going," Jason said, eager to be free from the musty, metallic smell.

Marie nodded in agreement. She gazed at the ground as they hurried over it, freezing when something captured her attention. "Jason! Look!" She pointed to the imprints that lay on the soil staring up at her. "They're theirs, right? Right?"

Jason scanned the footprints. "Julian," he said. He turned toward the second pair, analyzing it.

"Is it Will?"

Jason's smile faltered. "They're hurt," he said, "or at least one of them is hurt really badly. Look at all this blood!" He turned around, the sight circling him, emphasizing his point. "Julian was injured before he disappeared but not this much." Jason's eyes trailed across the branches and down the trunks, ending at the mushy soil.

"We have to find them." Marie shuddered and edged closer to Jason. "We have to find them," she repeated, "and soon."

They began to follow the tracks.

"Marie," Jason whispered, taking her hand and pulling her toward a looming tree. He brushed his hand against the trunk, studying the scarlet arrow that was drawn roughly on the bark.

"Julian?" Marie asked. Her eyes were wide with surprise.

Jason shook his head. "Before he disappeared, Julian was really out of it. Under normal circumstances, I wouldn't doubt that it was him …"

"But?"

"But," Jason continued hesitantly, "it's not a normal circumstance, is it?" He managed a wry smile before it faded. "I'm pretty sure Julian has a concussion—which means your brother should be behind this."

"What about Diego? Or Mr. Razat?"

"These aren't their footprints," said Jason. "They have larger feet."

Marie was torn between relief and anxiety.

Jason loosely wrapped an arm around her bruised shoulders and led her away, glancing down at the footprints in front of them.

"Jason?" asked Marie suddenly. She pointed to the patch of dirt in front of them, the prints branching off toward a bush.

Jason's eyes followed the frantic tracks. "William and Jule—they found something."

Marie watched over his shoulder as Jason crept nearer and cautiously peered over the bush. He gasped in surprise and stumbled back, a look of alarm flashing across his face.

Marie briefly saw a limp hand before Jason blocked the sight. "Jason?"

Jason's face was paler than before, and the dark circles around his eyes contrasted tremendously against his skin. "It's Mr. Razat and Diego," he said softly. He was still staring at the bush.

Marie gulped and turned around. She froze when she heard a quiet but unmistakable sound.

It was a soft swoosh over the ground, a noise that would go unnoticed by anyone in a forest full of groans and creaks—a forest full of sounds. To Jason and Marie, it was the sound of death approaching.

"It's coming," Marie whispered. She exchanged a look of horror with Jason.

He scrambled toward Marie and grabbed her hand, breaking into a sprint. "Hurry!"

"What about—"

"They're dead!"

They turned a corner sharply, colliding with a rocky wall that knocked the breath out of them both. Marie struggled to her feet, planting her hands on her knees as she attempted to regain her breath. "We can't keep running," she panted.

"We have to—"

"No," insisted Marie. "*I* can't keep running!"

Jason anxiously glanced around the area and pointed to a small opening between two large and jagged rocks.

"A cave then?" he suggested, and without waiting for an answer, he grabbed her hand and tugged her toward the opening. He dropped to his knees, easily fitting through the crack.

Marie followed in hesitation. As she entered the dark tunnel, she bit her lip, peering into the darkness that surrounded her. "Jason?" She reached forward with her hands to feel how wide the burrow was.

"Over here."

Marie hurried after his floating voice.

"Are you okay?" Jason asked.

"So far."

"I think this leads to a larger cavern; it slopes uphill from here."

They reached the end together, and Marie edged herself out of the hole first, cautiously lowering her foot until it met with something solid.

A loud crack echoed around them, sending shivers that raced up Marie's spine. As she stepped out, the sound ensued several times. She frowned in disgust as a strong, musky smell assaulted her—the stench like rotting eggs and animal guts. Behind her, she heard Jason step down and groan in revulsion.

"Let's get some light," he muttered. "Come on, help me." He clutched Marie's hand through the darkness. Together they made it to a wall and began to search for any loose rocks.

Jason pried some free, and a thin shaft of light beamed down.

Marie's hands were next to his, scratching at the rocks frantically. Holes spurted from the seemingly solid wall, and at last, they were rewarded with a broad sunray that shone down on them.

"Finally," Marie sighed, trying to breathe in the clean and unscented air. "Jason?" Marie asked when Jason remained silent. She turned around. Her hands flew to her mouth, and she gagged dreadfully, shoving her back to the wall.

The cavern was littered with bones, some gleaming a soft but pure white, others dirtied with brown and yellow and red. *Human skulls* stared up at them, smiling blankly at the couple. *Blood* stained the gray walls, painting the rocks crimson. *Limbs* were scattered, the flesh slowly rotting off. *They were in the plant's lair.*

❈

Julian sighed, leaning against one of the trees closer to him.

William mirrored his action as he cradled his injured arm. "Are you hurt badly?"

Julian shook his head and groaned when that resulted in a wave of dizziness. "Your arm?" he asked as he tried to recover.

William glanced at the bloodied slashes. "It'll be fine."

"We should leave another sign in case someone comes this way."

William shivered slightly before running a finger down his arm, wetting it with blood. He frowned with disgust before painting an arrow onto a tree trunk. "Thanks for saving me back there," he said quietly. "It's my fault you're injured this much."

"No it's not," said Julian. "I was hurt before I found you."

William caught sight of Julian's wrapped wrist and winced. "Did you do that?"

"Jason."

"You two are like brothers, right?"

"No, we are not *like* brothers," said Julian intensely, "we *are* brothers. Blood doesn't matter. We care about each other like a family; we *are* a family."

"Can I ask you something?"

"You could ask, but I won't guarantee an answer."

"I wanted to ask you about your past." William shifted, seemingly ashamed of his question. "Remember when that plane flew over us? And Jason and you told us how you guys met? Well, after—"

"I heard."

"You heard?" William repeated in a quiet whisper.

"I wasn't sleeping. Since then, I've been wondering when you or Marie were going to ask me something. I'm actually surprised it took this long."

"So you're going to tell me?"

Julian smiled sadly. "My mother was an only child, and her parents died when she was young—like me. My father's parents were the owners of a large company in England. They were murdered on a trip to Japan."

"All right," said William, "but why are you telling me this?"

"To understand, you need to know the basics. My father brought the company from England to North America but was later forced to sell it." Julian's smile faded. "That's when it all went downhill."

"You can really remember all of this?" asked William.

"Well, I can't remember *all* of it. A few years after Ken and Emily adopted me, I began digging for information about my family. Most of this information I got out of old newspapers and the few relatives who were willing to talk to me.

"After my father's company was bought out, he began to drink. And when he drank, he got violent." Julian shuddered. "This part I can remember clearly. He'd hurt my sister—"

"Madison?"

"He'd hurt Madison and my mother, and he'd make me watch. If I tried to do anything about it, he'd only hurt them more. After a year, my mother told him she was taking us and leaving. She had had enough." Julian smiled. "For *one* year, our lives were perfect. We weren't very wealthy, but we were happy. We weren't scared to come home anymore. But after that year, he told my mom he had changed and begged her to come back. He told her exactly what she wanted to hear, and she believed everything he said."

"So he changed?"

"For the first few weeks. And then it began again, and instead of interfering, my mother pretended nothing happened. She would look the other way when he raised his hand; she would never acknowledge the bruises or blood; she refused to believe things had gone back to the way they were before. She became hollow and lifeless, someone completely different than the mother I used to love.

"The neighbors would always ignore the screams that came from our house. They had asked about it once or twice, but my father always claimed he had difficulty hearing, and so he liked to turn the volume on the television set really high, and they believed him.

"One day, my mother snapped. She ran into the room as he was hurting us, and they began to fight. I grabbed Madison and pulled her into my room. I tried to stop the bleeding." Julian looked at his hands and rubbed his fingers together. "There was so much blood. And I could hear my mother screaming and pleading and *begging* him to stop. But that monster just laughed."

"He killed her?"

Julian nodded. "He came into my room and grabbed me and Madison. He pulled us into the kitchen and threw us onto her. I tried to get to the phone because I remembered before she changed she had told me if anything happened to her, *call 911*. But he caught me before I could, and he locked me in the closet. I watched him kill Madison, watched him as he watched her life fade from her eyes."

"What happened after?"

"He *laughed*," whispered Julian. "He laughed and opened the closet and pushed me toward her body. He forced me to clean the blood from the floor and walls. When he wasn't looking, I grabbed the phone and locked myself in the bathroom. I called 911 and told them everything while he was trying to break down the door."

"Did he?"

"Eventually, but by then I was on the roof. I had climbed up there from the window. I saw the sirens from a distance and told him he was going to get what he deserved. That was when he began to bash his head into the bathroom wall. After the police found me, they were hesitant to bring me down."

"And you were eight when all of this happened?"

"Hard to believe, isn't it?"

❊

"Hurry!" Marie cried, digging at the rocks in front of her with renewed strength.

They had finally made an opening that both could fit through, and Marie was the first one to scramble out of the cavern. She gasped deeply, sucking in fresh air. She moved to the side as Jason stumbled through, clinging to the soil in desperation.

"We're out," Jason whispered, rolling onto his back. He glanced back at the hole, and a hand flew to his mouth. "I think I'm going to be sick," he mumbled before scrambling toward the closest clump of bushes.

Marie could hear him retching before her own stomach started to churn. Gagging, she was driven to her hands and knees as she struggled with the vile lump that had risen in her throat. She fell to the side, turning sharply so that she didn't land in the mess she had just created.

"Marie?" a weak voice called out.

She forced herself to stand. "Over here," she responded, surprised to hear how frail she sounded. She found Jason with his head pressed between his knees. He looked up, his forehead covered in sweat and his pale skin glistening. "Are you okay?"

Marie shook her head. "I think *I* should be the one asking that."

"Just give me a minute," he muttered, breathing deeply.

Marie nodded and sat next to him, wiping her mouth with the back of her hand. The bitter taste of vomit was the only thing she was aware of.

After a long moment of silence Jason looked up. "Let's go."

"Are you sure you'll be all right?"

"Does it make a difference? We still need to get moving."

"It's getting dark, Jason," said Marie as she followed after him. "What if we don't find them, and they have to spend the night alone and injured!"

"We will find them."

"No!" exclaimed Marie in frustration. "Jason, actually *think* about it! They're out there, obviously injured! They might not be able to defend themselves if the plant decides to make an appearance! It's hard enough to spot it in the daylight; what about when the sun goes down?"

"We'll find them before then."

"We might not—"

"I know!" Jason snapped. He faced her, and the intensity of his glare softened. "I know," he repeated with an air of desperation. "But they will survive; they have to."

"Jason?" asked Marie again.

"Marie?" he mimicked.

"How will I find Julian? I mean, if we get home—"

"When."

"*When* we get home, we'll be separated. I don't want to be separated. I think I love him."

"Twenty-four, Dacanto Street. Look us up *when* we get home."

"Jason—"

"Wait!" Jason interrupted frantically. "Do you hear that?" His face lit up, and he roughly grabbed Marie by her shoulders. "Voices!" he shouted gleefully, "voices!"

"What?" said Marie in bewilderment.

"Voices!" repeated Jason excitedly. "Don't you hear them?" He sprinted down the path, leaving Marie behind.

"Jason!" Marie cried out in shock. She began to pump her legs, trying to catch up with the swift teenager. She soon lost sight of him and collapsed on her hands and knees, struggling to catch her breath. "Jason!" she screamed desperately. She shuffled backward until she braced against a looming tree. She curled into a ball, clutching at her knees as she sobbed uncontrollably. "Don't leave me!"

No one answered.

17

Jason skidded to a stop, breathing heavily as he struggled to still his shaking body. The voices had led him this far and then vanished. He was briefly aware that he had abandoned Marie to the murderous forest. He couldn't justify his actions, but the voices had stirred the ashes of hope inside him, slowly but steadily kindling an old fire to life.

"Is anyone there?" he yelled, straining his already hoarse voice.

No answer greeted him, and suddenly Jason was hit with a wave of despair. He kicked the base of the tree, wincing when the front of his toe smashed against the rough bark.

"Hello?"

Jason froze, and his eyes widened in shock. He opened his mouth and then closed it without a sound.

"Hello? Is somebody there?"

"Over here!" Jason cried out. "Where are you?"

"Follow my voice," a man strictly commanded.

Jason was shaking with disbelief as he quickly brushed his tears away. He stepped through a curtain of vines and came face-to-face with a middle-aged man. The man had stern lines etched into his face, and an odd twinkle glittered in his left eye.

"Who are you?"

"Lieutenant Larose."

"I'm Jason." They shook hands. "How did you find us?"

"A plane passed by here a few days ago. The pilot saw your fire and signaled us. We came as soon as we could."

"You're real, right? I'm not delusional …"

Lieutenant Larose chucked deeply. "You're not delusional, kid. I'm real flesh and blood."

Jason smiled in relief. "How'd you see the island in the dark?"

"The fire you lit guided us here," Lieutenant Larose replied.

"Fire?" Jason repeated before he gasped. He grabbed the man's hand, trying to turn him around. "The others! We have to find them. Marie and William and Jule!"

"I've sent out a search team. Whoever's here, we'll find them." The man gently pried Jason's hand from his and then took a solid grip on his arm.

"No!" exclaimed Jason. "They'll die! There's something that kills people. We have to find them *now*!" Jason wrenched his hand from Lieutenant Larose and slammed the edge of his palm the man's face. He took off, leaving the man clutching at his broken nose in shock.

❂

"William?" Julian called out. The sun was slowly descending, and darkness was beginning to pierce the sky. "William!" Julian stepped forward and accidentally hooked his foot around a loose root, tumbling to the ground. His head collided with the base of a tree, sending a wave of agony that shot through his nerves. Groaning, he struggled to sit up and tried to blink away the sudden dizziness.

"Julian?"

"Jason?" Julian answered skeptically. He squinted past the shadowed trees, trying to peer through the black fog that cloaked the forest. He stumbled to his feet and swayed drastically.

"Where are you?"

"I'm not sure," Julian muttered suspiciously. "Jason, what—"

Something lightly brushed against his hands, tickling his skin. Julian jumped in terror and whirled around, once more losing his footing. Hands caught him before he could hit the ground.

"Jule!"

Julian stared into Jason's starlit face before throwing his arms around him tightly. "Jason, remind me if we ever get off this island to—"

"We've been rescued!"

Julian froze at the words. He felt numb at the very thought of going home.

"The fire you and Will lit guided them here."

"I didn't light any fires, Jase." Julian gasped and grabbed Jason's shoulder with surprising strength for his injured condition. "William! He must've done it! We found Mr. Razat and Diego, and the matches were sticking out of Mr. Razat's pocket, and we couldn't just leave them there because—"

"William? He's not with you?"

"Not anymore."

Jason squared his shoulders. His posture was tense and rigid. "I have to find him, Jule."

"No!" Julian exclaimed. He tightened his grip. "I won't lose you again!"

"He might be in trouble."

"The rescue people can find him!" said Julian. "You stay with me."

"Julian, I can't—"

"You go, and you might never come back—never, Jason! *Never!*"

"Jule," Jason whispered. "If I don't make it back—"

"Don't!" cried Julian. "Just … don't."

"If I don't make it back," repeated Jason, "I want you to tell everyone—Emily, Ken, and Jesse—especially Jesse—that I love them, and I'll always be with them in here." Jason pressed his palm against Julian's heart.

"Jason, don't—"

"And make sure my brother knows how much I love him, and that I'll always miss him after everything we've been through."

"Jesse?" whispered Julian. "He'll miss you too."

Jason squeezed Julian's arms lightly before leaning closer. "Not Jesse," whispered Jason before he let go of Julian.

"Jason!" Julian shrieked after him. He leaned against the tree beside him for support and tried to follow. An arm encircled his waist and held him back.

"Let me go!" Julian screamed as he beat his fist against the offending arms.

"Calm down, son," someone said. "My name is Dane Mailto. I'm part of the Dalia's Rescue Team."

Julian ignored the man and began to kick his feet wildly, trying to push the arms away from his stomach. "Let me go!" He thrashed violently, clawing at the limbs that secured him. "Jason! Jason, come back!"

"Cane, he's struggling!"

"What am I supposed to do?"

"Help me!"

Julian felt someone pull his fingers away from the man's arm.

"Calm down—"

"Jason!" Julian cried, ignoring the two men.

"Who's Jason?"

"Let's just bring him back. The girl said there were still three alive."

"Alive? Why would they be dead?"

"Let's just get him back before he loses it again." The man pulled a small communicator from his pocket. "Lieutenant," he muttered over the static, "we've found another one."

※

Marie sat hunched over as she stared, transfixed, at the dancing embers that swirled in front of her. A little to her left a large helicopter stood proudly, its shiny metal glimmering through the darkness.

A man old enough to be her father took a seat next to her in the sand; she could feel his eyes study her worn expression. He had several bandages wrapped around his nose; blood was beginning to seep through.

"My men have found another person and are escorting him back as we speak." Lieutenant Larose let out a long breath. "Now, are you going to tell me what happened? I doubt all those injuries are from the crash."

"You wouldn't believe me if I told you." An awkward air of silence settled over them, and Marie resorted to studying the lines etched in her palms.

"Let go of me!"

"Julian," whispered Marie. She stood but her knees nearly buckled as her vision began to spot black.

"Easy there," Lieutenant Larose commented, steadying Marie before she could fall.

Marie shook her head and pushed him away, running toward Julian. "Let him go!" she cried.

Lieutenant Larose nodded in agreement. The men acknowledged his nod and released Julian.

"He wouldn't," Julian muttered and wrapped his arms around himself.

Marie dropped to his level and grabbed his hands. "Who wouldn't?"

"Jason."

"He's not dead, is he? Julian? That's your name, right?" Lieutenant Larose stared at Julian with an unbearably calm façade.

"You've come to save us?" asked Julian. "How?"

"A plane saw a fire around here a few days ago—"

"It's only been a few days since then?" asked Julian. "It feels as though months have gone by."

"It's been about three weeks since you crashed. A plane saw a fire coming from one of the islands. All of the islands around here are uninhabited, and so we assumed said island was sporting the fourteen North Americans that had gone missing."

"People were," Julian paused, "people were looking for us?"

"Looking for you?" repeated Lieutenant Larose. "You wouldn't believe the trouble that's been going on since you all just vanished! The media's been going crazy. Things have been going wild ever since you all disappeared." Lieutenant Larose dug into his pocket, pulling out a crisply folded paper. "I've got a list of names. I'll read them out, and you two can tell me who we still need to find."

Marie's smile disappeared. "There's no need for that," she said evenly. "You can cross out my name and Julian's, and start searching for Jason and William."

Lieutenant Larose frowned, lines crinkling on his forehead. "Am I expected to believe that out of sixteen, only four of you survived?"

"It'll only be two if you don't get a move on."

Lieutenant Larose suddenly began to look at the duo in suspicion. "There were sixteen of you in the beginning, and now there's only you two?"

"Don't you dare," Marie said quietly.

"It's not looking good."

"You think *we* killed everyone? You think we *killed* everyone?"

"Look, I'm just saying—"

"No!" interrupted Marie with a cry. Lividly, she stepped forward, ready to challenge his accusations. "One of those people was our captain, and he died from a stroke! Three of those people are—*were* my family. Two others were my friends and *their* family. And the other three were Julian and Jason's best friends. How can you possibly *think* we killed them? In the time we spent together here, we *became* a family. And families don't kill each other." Marie never saw the grimace that flashed across Julian's face.

"I'm just trying to understand what happened," said Lieutenant Larose wearily.

"Sir!" one man called out as he emerged from the forest with an alarming speed. He reached the fire panting. "Sir?"

"Methyl," Lieutenant Larose said. They saluted before a panicked expression flew across Methyl's face.

"Requesting—"

"Agreed," Lieutenant Larose interrupted impatiently.

Methyl's sympathetic glance did not go unnoticed by the two teenagers. "We found two others, sir."

"Condition?"

"One is in a coma, sir. The other is dead."

"What?" Marie shrieked. Then she saw the body two men were carrying out of the forest.

"Jason!" Julian whispered. He was trembling.

Two of the soldiers gently lowered the body to the ground.

Julian followed, pressing his hands against Jason's cheeks in a futile attempt to wake him.

"I'm sorry," one man said, but his comment went unheard.

Julian frantically grabbed Jason's hand and closed his eyes. "He's alive!" His smile quickly faded as he twisted around. "Why are you standing around? Help him! He's still alive!"

"I'm sorry, sir, but—"

"Why do you keep saying that?" Julian demanded. "Stop being sorry! He's not dead!"

"Get him away from the body," Lieutenant Larose commanded.

Marie glared at him. "Let Julian stay. They're brothers!"

Lieutenant Larose turned to her. "He's not going to make it, and I don't want Julian to have a breakdown. Nothing's more traumatic than seeing someone close to you dead. And if they're brothers, then that's worse."

"Traumatic?" Marie repeated, ready to laugh in his face. "You have no idea what traumatic is." She gasped suddenly, a choked sound worming its way past her lips. "William!" Hands grabbed at her wrists, stopping her before she could reach her brother. "Will!" she screamed, kicking her feet angrily. She faced Lieutenant Larose with agony splayed across her fair features. "Don't do this," she pleaded, "let me see him."

"You don't want to see him like this," said Lieutenant Larose before beckoning a handful of men forward. "Escort our survivors into the helicopter. See if you can clean them up a bit."

Marie let herself be pulled away, gazing at Lieutenant Larose in misery.

❋

Marie stared at the blank stars stretched out in front of her, no longer shimmering mockingly. The gray clouds hung in the air as if held by invisible strings that swayed side to side. The rocky shore below became smaller and smaller, until it was just another dot mixed into the earth. Marie tried not to turn around, knowing that behind the line of men lay William.

Julian sat on the opposite side. His face was void of emotion, and his eyes gazed vacantly ahead. His cheeks were stained with tears, old and new. In his hand, he clutched Jason's sweater, something he had snatched from one of the men's hands.

Lieutenant Larose pushed his way past another herd of men before taking a seat facing both teenagers.

"Well," he began, "we have a couple of hours before we reach where we're headed. Other than that, I have a question that I think you two can clear up for me." Lieutenant Larose shifted closer so that he was leaning on his knees and staring down at them. "Who is Thomas Derka?"

"Thomas?" repeated Marie softly. She traced the glass window with the tips of her fingers before leaning her head against the pane. She glanced across the aisle toward Julian. "We were supposed to go scuba diving. He was our instructor."

Lieutenant Larose quickly scribbled something on the paper he held. "What happened to Thomas?"

"We never saw him after the crash," said Marie. "We assumed he was dead."

"But you have no proof," said Lieutenant Larose.

Marie shook her head, immediately picking up the man's trail of thought. Instead of challenging his unspoken theory, she forced herself to remain quiet.

Lieutenant Larose rose and disappeared among his men once more, camouflaging with the similar colors around them.

Marie shot a fleeting look at Julian, worried about how unresponsive he was. His knuckles were pale and white as snow as he clutched Jason's torn sweater desperately.

Marie couldn't believe they were finally going home, after all the suffering and misery they had endured, all the trials and struggles and the stress and trauma. She turned toward the stars and brushed her finger against the dirty glass, wishing to bring the dim lights closer. She gazed past the window and watched as soft, orange streaks broke through the clouds. The sky was decorated with pink, and the moon no longer radiated its silvery sheen. The sun was rising, slowly but *surely*.

Fear would be a thing of the past and hope a thing of the future.

18

Two months. That was the first time she had seen him since the island. It had been at William's funeral. They had waited to bury him—waited and waited until Marie couldn't pretend he was alive any longer.

She had been clothed in all black, a soft veil covering her pale and scarred face. At one moment of silence, she had looked up and caught the first glimpse of him, head bowed, hair cleanly washed and cut, face void of blood and dirt, and glasses sitting firmly on his face, reflecting the sunlight. She almost didn't recognize him. Their eyes had met briefly before he broke contact and disappeared among the crowd of mourners.

He was the first to lay his flower on William's coffin—a beautiful white flower that was different from all the rest. He walked like a king among commoners, and his pure rose shone brightly in the sea of red.

He left soon after, not bothering to find her, and it was probably for the best. After all, not once had she attempted to find him. She remembered his address clearly—Twenty-four, Dacanto Street.

She knew Jason's funeral had been a week ago, it had been mentioned on the news. She had made no attempt to go to the funeral service because she knew she couldn't face him for a while. He reminded her of the island, and all she wanted to do was forget.

The sun slowly entered Marie's new room with balanced grace, gently kissing her cheeks with a warm glow. Her eyes were already open, burning with the remains of another nightmare. The sun seemed to hiss as it grazed across her skin, revealing scars that seemed to be a new part of her.

A knock echoed through the room, followed by another. Marie faced the door silently. Her eyes were clouded in fatigue. The knob jiggled slightly, and the chestnut door was pushed open. Her aunt stood in the frame, worry evident in her posture. She stepped into the room and sat next to Marie.

"It's beautiful, isn't it?"

Marie shifted away from her and nodded. She didn't miss the look of hurt that flashed across her aunt's face. Marie sighed and slowly got to her feet.

"Where are you going?"

"To get breakfast."

Her aunt glanced at the clock but said nothing. Marie ignored her Aunt's look and walked to the hallway, carefully stepping down the slippery wooden steps.

"Would you like some pancakes?" Instead of waiting for a response, her aunt got out a frying pan and handed the mix to Marie. They worked in a comfortable silence for a moment before her Aunt ruined it. "Perry is going to see him today. Should I tell him you're coming?"

Marie froze, and the spoon she was holding slipped from her hand and clattered to the tiled floor. Neither paid the cutlery any attention. "I can't," she whispered. She tried to blink back the sudden onslaught of tears she could feel. "Not yet, it's too soon."

Her aunt left the frying pan and pulled her into a hug, squeezing tightly.

"Marie, it's been a month since Will's been buried."

Marie pulled her aunt back into a hug and pressed her face against her aunt's shoulder. "I can't," she repeated miserably. "It's too soon."

❈

Marie quickly slipped into the bathroom and sighed in relief as she locked the door. She glanced at the full-length mirror in front of her and bit her lip, rocking back and forth on her heels.

Quickly, she stripped to her underwear. It was only in here that she could wear the least amount of clothes without being self-conscience. Outside—where everyone could see her—she had to cover herself up.

Marie studied her legs first. Most of the scars had healed, but the ones that jumped out were the patterned holes wrapped around her shins. Her arms and hands were adorned with scratches mutilating the skin. Her scabs were bloody and disgusting, and every so often she was tempted to just pick them all off and be done with it. She couldn't wait for winter so that she'd have an excuse to wear gloves.

She raised her eyes before coming to a stop at her face. She fingered the tiny spot near her hairline.

Marie glanced at the clear jar that sat on the vanity. She grabbed it and quickly rubbed the sticky mixture onto her skin. The doctor had promised this would work, and Marie was willing to try anything to make the scars go away.

❀

Marie sighed, something she seemed to be doing a lot lately. She stared at the stack of books beside her but didn't touch—never touched.

She had discovered her aunt owned all his copies and had asked to borrow them. The next day, she found them stacked against her bed, and there they stayed, collecting dust. The guilt was slowly eating away at her, gnawing at her mind relentlessly. She liked the feeling; it made her feel something other than sorrow or pain.

Marie stood suddenly, grabbed her coat, donned her gloves, wrapped her scarf around her neck, and hurried down the stairs. As she passed the window she noticed the snow whirling around mercilessly.

"Marie?" her aunt called out from the kitchen, rushing into the hallway. "Where are you going?"

Marie bit her lip, trying not to lose her sudden spark of courage. "I'm ready."

"In this weather? It's a blizzard out there!"

"I've been through worse and lived," she pointed out acidly.

Her aunt grimaced but said nothing.

❀

It was pure coincidence really that they were buried right beside each other.

She had seen the dark figure from afar, clothed entirely in black. He stood out like a shining beacon in the harsh and ruthless snow, and as Marie approached, her heart began to thump loudly against her chest; she recognized him.

When she reached the two graves, she was still staring, and he finally turned around, meeting her eyes with that same surreal, calm expression he usually wore.

"Marie," he whispered softly.

She barely heard him over the roaring wind.

Marie faced her brother's grave, struggling not to cry. "Julian." She glanced at him and noticed more than one white rose propped against the tombstone. It was so like him. Marie burned a look into the white roses that sat beside her brother's grave, hating Julian for being so kind. They both gazed silently at the graves in front of them before Marie turned to him and exclaimed, "Twenty-four Dacanto Street." She could feel his confused eyes upon her and cringed when she felt her stomach churn. "Jason told me, and I never forgot."

"Why did you pretend?"

"I didn't know what to say," Marie said finally, badgering herself for the foolish excuse.

Julian turned around, revealing a small child hidden behind his leg.

"Who's that?" asked Marie, immediately drawing the worst conclusion.

"Jesse."

The child looked up, angry eyes staring at Marie. She was taken aback by the intensity of the glare; he reminded her of Jason. From the stories she had heard, Jesse was supposed to be a playful, carefree, and loving child, but what stood before her seemed to be the exact opposite.

"This is Marie," said Julian to the small child. "She was one of Jason's friends."

Marie noticed he didn't say she was one of *his* friends or perhaps more. Even though she expected it, the words cut deep into her heart.

"We missed the bus, Jule."

"Bus?" repeated Marie.

Julian nodded, clasping Jesse's hand and walking toward the front gate.

"Wait!" Marie exclaimed as an idea quickly formed in her head. "Why don't you guys come home with me? We can have a bite, and my uncle can ride you home later!"

"Sorry, Marie. Not today. Emily and Ken are expecting us back soon, and we've already missed our bus."

Marie watched as Julian and Jesse left the cemetery and vanished around the corner. She turned to her brother's grave, shaking with a mixture of cold and grief as she began to cry.

❈

The second time they met was much like the first, except this time it was in the middle of summer and raining—hard. Marie wasn't sure why she chose this time over all others to visit her brother; it just seemed right. She hadn't gone since the last time; she was afraid she would run into Julian again.

She had taken an umbrella, but with the wind present, it didn't offer her much protection. She stopped when she saw him—alone this time—and forced herself to remain calm. She approached the graves holding a crimson rose in one hand.

"Marie," he greeted as he laid white roses next to the withered ones on both graves. His umbrella shadowed his face, but she could imagine his ghostly smile.

"Julian," she responded, placing her flower beside her brother's grave. She had forgotten Jason, or at least that's what she told herself. "How are things?"

"As okay as they can be." He smiled. "I gave the necklace to the museum."

"That's good," Marie said evenly. "How much did you sell it for?"

"I didn't sell it," said Julian. "I *gave* it to them—for free."

"Well," said Marie awkwardly, struggling to keep a hold on her umbrella. "I guess I'll see you later?"

"I don't think you will," said Julian, and he left her standing there, mouth agape in surprise.

"Julian," exclaimed Marie before he could disappear. "I love you!"

He froze before looking over his shoulder, and a painful expression fluttered across his face.

"No, you don't," he said softly, "not anymore." He vanished through the front gate before Marie could respond, but he was right.

❊

Five years: that was how long it was until Marie saw him again—or saw him in person. He was always on the television, his new books being praised for an author so young. And every time he came on, Marie would curse and click power on the remote.

She had her own life now; nothing connected her to the past except for him, and as much as she wanted to, she couldn't break that small connection. She bought every single book he had written and started her own collection. But, like before, she never read them. They lay on her bookcase, collecting dust.

She had made the long trip from her new house, a forty-minute ride on the bus to get there. She had missed him all the other times she had visited, usually finding his white roses laid with great care next to both tombstones—an action she never copied—and it was obvious it was he who had the better heart.

It was a beautiful day, warm and bright, with no hint of rain present. She wore a summery dress, no longer self-conscious because all her scars had faded. The wind blew around her, and she loved how it felt. The breeze licked her skin as she walked briskly.

Her heart began to beat painfully against her chest when she saw him. He looked exactly as she had pictured—the perfect image of a wealthy, young bachelor.

"Marie," he greeted pleasantly, first as always.

She smiled at him. His hair was adorably messy, his glasses framed his green eyes, and his hands were jammed in his pockets.

"Julian," she said in return, placing her flowers next to her brother's grave. "How's everything?"

"Bit busy with my new book."

Marie wanted to tell him she knew. She wanted to tell him that she had every one of his books at home, waiting to be opened to a crisp page. But she didn't.

"That sounds fun," she said softly, bringing a hand from behind her back to brush away the hair that had gathered around her face and unconsciously revealing a ring she had sought to keep secret.

"You're married. Congrats!" He laughed and hugged her quickly.

"Thank you," Marie said in surprise, fingering the small diamond on her finger. "He was my doctor."

"Sounds like a good life," Julian said.

"Anyone for you?" she asked, hoping he would say yes. He didn't. "So I hear you're a big success," she stated casually, trying to start another conversation.

"I guess so."

She gulped before she faced him, covering her bare arms with her small hands. "Julian, what happened between us?"

"What do you mean?"

Marie shivered, no longer enjoying the biting wind around her. "We used to be so much in love, but then we just ... stopped."

"No," said Julian quietly. A familiar hollow gleam twinkled in his eyes. "You stopped. You've changed, and I don't like what you've changed into. The Marie I loved died when we left the island, and you're someone completely different."

And as he left, his words stabbed painfully at her heart, but she knew it was the truth.

Printed in the United States
149000LV00001B/26/P